NEW

MEMORIES

DEBORAH WALLACE

New Memories

Published by Deborah Wallace

ISBN 978-1-951457-07-5

Chapter 1

Sheriff Jake Hamilton drove down the highway, on his way to the station in Willow Ridge, Arkansas, noting the downed trees and branches from the thunder storm the previous night. The downpour had raged for hours and for once he hadn't been called out in it. He'd notify the highway department of the mess he passed. Fortunately, no trees totally blocked the road.

Halfway through the sharpest curve on his drive, a white patch caught his attention. He pulled off the road, flipped on his lights, and got out of the car.

A commercial van lay on its side down the embankment. He worked his way down the embankment, brush and ruts from the tires slowed him. About six feet down, the slope became steeper. The van must have flipped onto its side, flattening brush as it slid the rest of the way down, allowing him easier passage.

The van's roof was crushed against a tree, fortunately behind the passenger area. In front of the van, he peered through the windshield. No one hung from a seatbelt in the driver's seat and for a moment he thought any occupants had exited. In the shadows against the passenger door, he spotted a pale face, probably a woman or teen.

He lifted the walkie-talkie from his side to call the dispatcher. "Dannie?"

"Yeah, Sheriff?"

"Can you send an ambulance and wrecker to marker forty-seven on highway twelve?"

"There again? Right away, Jake."

At the back of the van, he tried to pull the doors open. The impact from the tree had jammed them.

Rounding the van, he eyed the underside. Choosing foot and hand holds, he worked his way up. Once sitting beside the driver's door, he noted that the company name had been covered with spray paint.

He peered through the window at the heap of woman resting on the passenger door with the side of her face against the glass, her eyes closed. From her coloring, she was still alive.

He maneuvered through the opening and rested a foot on the steering wheel, then placed a foot on the edge of the passenger seat beside the woman. He balanced between the seats.

Jake brushed her hair out of her face and found a faint but steady pulse on her neck. He brushed across bruises on her throat left by fingers, and tamped down the anger that swirled inside him. Her face was bruised and swollen, making it hard to guess her age, but probably no more than thirty. He couldn't tell if the injuries were caused by the accident or by whoever had choked her. A gash at her hairline had stopped bleeding. One hand was trapped under her and the other smeared with dried blood, and ringless.

She seemed to have been in a hurry, traveling without jacket or shoes. Maybe running from an abusive husband or boyfriend, and too rushed to buckle her seat belt.

Her dress was dirty and torn. It was bunched up mid thigh and he tugged down the hem to preserve her modesty.

Without knowing what kind of injuries she had, he couldn't move her.

He removed his jacket, draped it over the woman and tucked it around her. "My name's Jake. Stay with me. Help is on the way."

He slid his hand under the coat and took the woman's

hand. Her hand was so small in his, the fingers delicate.

He hated going to domestic abuse calls. So many times he'd haul away the man and the woman took him back. He'd try to be compassionate as he explained the help that was available, and let them know there were people who cared what happened to them.

Gently squeezing this woman's hand, he examined her face. Again he wondered if she'd run from whoever had injured her. No other reason explained how she was dressed.

"I'll make sure you're taken care of. I'll keep you safe." He didn't know if she could hear him, but hoped his voice comforted her. Sirens became audible in the distance. "The ambulance is almost here. We'll have you out real soon."

Within a few minutes the siren stopped, doors slammed closed and voices came closer, alerting Jake to people coming down the hill.

Someone banged on the hood of the van. The town had two EMT teams. Rob was the senior member. "Hey, Rob. Who's with you?"

"Walter. How's our patient?"

Jake glanced at her and back to Rob. "She's unconscious, breathing on her own, pulse faint but steady. I didn't want to move her in case she has spinal injuries. How do you want to get her out of here?"

"We'll have Henry open the back." He called up the hill to the driver of the wrecker. "Hey, Henry, can you bring down the jaws?"

Henry yelled back. "Be right there."

A minute later an engine roared to life. A few minutes after that, metal on metal clanked in the back of the van. The walls around him vibrated. A sliver of light showed between the back doors. It widened until one door popped and the men pulled the bottom door open.

Rob set his medical box inside, pushed it and scrambled

in behind it. Crouching, he made his way to the seats.

"Sheriff, I want you to come out of there."

Jake stepped down so he was behind the seat then stepped behind Rob.

Rob reached to the side of the seat and pushed the lever to lower the back of the seat.

Jake leaned over Rob's shoulder watching him inspect the woman. He felt her pulse, flashed a light in her eyes and checked for broken bones.

"Jake, can you hand me that neck brace?"

Jake complied and waited for it to be fitted. "How is she?"

"Hearts a little slow, but steady. She's breathing fine. Eyes are responsive. There's a bump on her head." He called out. "Hey, Walter, send in the backboard."

Jake grabbed the board as it came through the opening.

Rob patted the side door behind the seat. "Now set it down here." He explained how they were to move her and soon they slid her onto the backboard, then Rob strapped her down.

"Let's move."

Jake lifted his end and stepped backwards. She hardly weighed anything. For the first time, he noticed how thin she was. He and Rob carried the woman up the hill and put her in the ambulance.

Rob sat down beside her. "I'm going to start fluids. Walter, call it in."

Jake watched for a few seconds. "Take care of her."

Rob eyed him. "Sure thing, Sheriff."

Jake closed the door. It bothered him that the woman's feet were bare. He scrambled back to the van, and shone his flashlight around, not finding shoes, jacket or a purse. No personal items. He crawled out of the van, pulled out his cell phone and called his dispatcher. "Dannie, I need you to check a plate for me. He rattled off the number and gave a description of the van."

"Got it, Sheriff."

The motor wined as Henry dragged the cable from the wrecker down the hill to the van.

"Henry, there's something fishy about this. I want you to take the van over to the police garage so Mike can look it over."

"Will do, Sheriff."

He stared at the van, wonder why a woman in her condition was driving a commercial van on a night like last night.

Chapter 2

Jake popped the last bite of his sandwich into his mouth. He preferred his housekeeper's leftovers from the night before, but an occasional sandwich was fine. Abby's spicy chili the night before had been as good as usual, so there wasn't any left after the ranch hands finished the meal.

He sat back and drained his coffee as the phone rang. "Sheriff Hamilton."

"Hi, Sheriff. This is Dr. Caldwell. I was in the ER when the woman you found was brought in. We're calling her Jane Doe for now. I think you should come down here."

"Is she conscious?"

"Not yet, but we need to discuss her condition."

"All right. I'll be right there. What floor are you on?"

"Third, just ask for me at the nurses' station."

All the way to the hospital Jake turned over in his head what the doctor needed to discuss that he wouldn't tell him over the phone. Maybe the doctor had found more injuries than Jake had noticed.

Jake's step faltered when he saw the nurse with short red hair at the station. He stopped in front of her and waited for her to finish writing on a chart. She propped her elbow on the desk and rested her chin on it, blinked her pretty green eyes at him. "Hi, Sheriff. How's that ranch of yours?"

"It's good, Liz. I'm looking for Dr. Caldwell." He glanced down the hall.

"My sister's having a party this weekend. Want to join me?"

He turned back to her. "Uh, sorry, Liz. I already have plans." He'd made the mistake of having one date with her. It had been a torturous evening. She'd only talked about her exes and how they'd wronged her. He didn't need to do that again.

"Where can I find Dr. Caldwell?"

She sighed. "He's in room three-twelve with Jane Doe."

"Thanks." Jake walked past the desk, checking room numbers, his mind already on the woman he'd helped earlier.

Stepping into the room, Jake first saw the woman lying in the bed. Tubes connected to her arms, the skin that wasn't bruised was deathly pale. A steady beep reassured him that she was alive. Dr. Caldwell looped his stethoscope over his neck and approached Jake, holding up his hand to stop Jake from speaking. They stepped into the hallway. "Let's go down to the office."

Jake had talked to the doctor a number of times on cases. He cared about his patients and tended to talk to them like an uncle. Although he wasn't old, his brown hair was thinning. The doctor was one of the few men Jake had to look up to when they talked.

The doctor led him to a room behind the nurse's station and shut the door. He sat down and pointed to a chair for Jake. The doctor leaned forward, resting his arms on his thighs and whooshed out his breath.

"Where should I begin? I've never seen a woman in her condition and I've worked in the ER eight years."

A shiver went down Jake's spine. "Go on."

Dr. Caldwell glanced at his chart. "Her wrists look like they've been handcuffed for more than a few days, some raw skin but some partially healed. She's been badly beaten, probably several times over days or weeks."

Jake tightened his lips into a grim line. He'd arrested his share of abusive husbands and boyfriends, but none of the victims had been handcuffed. He hadn't noticed the marks, but then he remembered the blood that had covered her hand and arm.

Jake frowned. "There was dried blood on her hand."

The doctor nodded. "It wasn't hers. She only had the small cut on her forehead and it wouldn't have splattered like that. Your detective sent it out to be tested."

"Alex Brandt?"

"Yes."

He read from his folder. "She has two cracked ribs that have started to heal. She's got too many bruises to count in all stages of healing. She has a possible concussion and a sprained wrist, probably from the accident. There are bruises on her neck where she's been choked. There was bruising on her inner thighs and we found vaginal trauma. We used a rape kit and I've sent it to be tested. You should get the results in forty-eight hours."

Dr. Caldwell sat back in his chair and closed his eyes for a moment. He shook his head. "It's unbelievable what people will do to other people." He rubbed his forehead.

"I face the same thing. I take an abusive husband away so the wife has a chance to get out, but it doesn't happen as often as it should." Jake's face grew grimmer. "At least this woman chose to escape."

Dr. Caldwell rattled his papers. "There's more. The bottoms of her feet have cuts and imbedded gravel. She must have run barefoot."

Jake nodded.

"She has scratches on her back. The really strange thing is—"

"With all that, you can say something is strange?"

"Yeah. Her back is covered in scars. It looks like she's been whipped. They're probably years old."

"That poor woman must have had a life of hell." Old

scars and new bruises.

"One more thing. She suffered a miscarriage just after she came in. She was about three months. Probably caused by the accident. I've arranged a psychologist see her as soon as she wakes up."

He remembered how his housekeeper had initially reacted around men when she left her ex-husband. "A female psychologist."

The doctor nodded. "Yes, of course. Dr. Stacey Reynolds has worked wonders with battered women. I'll send her the file."

"Good." Jake stood. "I want to be called when she regains consciousness."

"Of course, Sheriff. I forgot to mention that the detective took her dress for analysis. That's all she was wearing."

"All right. Thanks."

Jake headed for the elevator and changed his mind, turning back to the woman's room. He touched her hand, and had a strong desire to protect her.

His grandfather had ingrained in him the importance of respecting women and treating them well. He never knew his grandmother, but knew so much about her by how lovingly his grandfather spoke of her. His grandfather and father taught him to respect his mother and sister, too. Not always easy with a know-it-all sister who was two years older.

Jake closed his eyes and drew in a breath as he remembered how his sister died at the hands of the man who professed to love her. She wouldn't listen to her twenty-two year old brother when he tried to convince her to leave her boyfriend. Too few listened.

"Hi, sunshine. It's Jake. I'm going to find who did this to you and make sure it never happens again."

Back at his car, he called dispatch. "Dannie, what do you have for me on the van?"

"Sheriff, the plates were stolen about a month ago."

"Call Mike and get the VIN from him. Hopefully, you'll have better luck with that."

"I'm on it."

~~~

Jake walked into the police garage. The white van sat in the farthest of the four bays, with all its doors open. Mike leaned into the back of the van and straightened up with a swab in his hand. He capped it as Jake crossed the floor. Mike did minor repairs to the police cars as well as forensics on the occasional suspicious vehicle.

"Mike, have you found anything?"

"Hi, Jake. The only fingerprints I found are in the driver's area. They're probably the girl's, but I haven't gotten her prints yet. There's some blood in the back that's been there a while." He waved the swab. "There are also some long strands of dark hair."

Jake nodded. "The woman has long, dark hair."

"I'll let you know if I find anything useful."

"Thanks, Mike. Let Alex know, too." Alex Brandt had become a good friend in the two years Alex had lived in Willow Ridge. He was a good detective, but Jake still didn't know why Alex decided to leave his busy life in Cleveland.

Upstairs, in the station, he stopped in front of the dispatcher. "Dannie, did you find anything?"

She ran a hand through her cropped blonde hair. "Oh, yeah. The van was stolen over three months ago in upstate New York."

A cold shiver went up Jake's spine. It was possible the poor woman had been subjected to torture for over three months. He hoped not, but she'd spent some amount of time being tortured. "Okay. Call Alex, give him the info. Have him contact the jurisdiction and let them know we have the van and get as much info as he can about its disappearance."

"Will do, Sheriff."

Chapter 3

The next morning, Jake stopped at the nurses' station. The petite, dark haired nurse pulled a folder from a stack on the desk and pushed it into a slot before picking up another.

"Hi, Beth. Any change in Jane Doe?"

She shook her head. "No, Sheriff. Sorry. The same as yesterday."

"Thanks." Jake strode down to Jane Doe's room. Normally, he'd called when he got into the office to check on a patient's status. He didn't know why he hadn't. He needed to see her, make sure she was all right. He stood beside her bed. The swelling was less pronounced today, revealing prominent cheekbones. He was tempted to touch her cheek. It was probably not something the sheriff should do.

She wasn't as pale as the day before, but the bruise on her forehead was darker. She must have gotten that one in the accident.

He rested his hand on hers and jumped at the voiced from the doorway. "Morning, Sheriff."

Jake spun around and the doctor raised an eyebrow.

"Hi, Dr. Caldwell. Can we talk in the hall?"

Jake pulled the door mostly closed. "Doctor, is it bad that she's still unconscious?"

"I'm not worried about it yet. Her scans were fine. She's been through a lot of trauma. Her body and mind need time to heal."

He nodded. After what she'd been through, maybe she didn't want to wake up.

~~~

Dannie waved to Jake when he entered the station. "Sheriff, Alex called. He didn't get any more relevant information on the van. It was stolen from Monticello, New York. The owner went out one morning and it was gone from his driveway."

"Thanks, Dannie."

Once in his office, Jake ran a missing persons search for the area surrounding Monticello. He spent an hour trying different parameters and gradually increasing the search radius, but couldn't find a match. He sat back and laced his fingers.

He assumed the van was stolen near where the woman went missing. If that was the case, then no one had filed a report.

He changed the search to their surround area and still came up blank.

He wondered if there was no one who cared about her enough to file a missing person report. Well, now she had one person who did, and he was going to make sure she stayed safe.

~~~

Jake walked into Jane Doe's room. He'd been stopping in morning and night for six days. He didn't know if she sensed that he was there and could hear him. He stared at her. She'd changed over the week. The bruising was barely perceptible. The marks on her neck were fading, but still visible. The smudges under her eyes had faded. Her top lip was a little too thin but it suited her. He wondered if she smiled much, but with what he knew of her, expected that she didn't.

He was first on scene at many accidents and didn't feel drawn to those victims. Maybe he cared so much because no one else did. He was compelled to visit her, talk to her, hold her hand. Deep down, he felt that she needed him. He took her hand.

"Good morning, sunshine. It's Jake." He spent some time telling her about the town and what he wanted to show her.

He was surprised when she squeezed his hand. He continued talking to her, encouraging her to wake up, but her hand relaxed, and no matter what else he said, she remained asleep.

Jake hurried to the nurses' station and asked if Dr. Caldwell was nearby.

Behind him the doctor said, "Why am I not surprised to see you, Sheriff?"

"Hi, Dr. Caldwell. I was holding Jane Doe's hand and talking to her and she squeezed mine. Does that mean something?"

"She may have started working her way up out of the coma. We'll keep closer tabs on her today."

"Thanks, Doc."

Jake drove to the station on autopilot. He hoped to soon find out who she was, and get answers to his questions. He hoped Jane Doe would make a full recovery from the emotional trauma she'd experienced. If she allowed him, he'd do whatever he could to help.

It sunk in that Dannie was calling him. He snapped his head toward her. Dannie waved folders like she was trying to get his attention.

"What are those?"

Dannie huffed. "Finally. Jake, you've got three lab reports related to Jane Doe."

"Thanks, Dannie. I hope they're more helpful than what

we've had so far. Did Alex get them, too?" At her nod, he grabbed a cup of coffee on the way to his office. He sat and fanned the folders on his desk. He was almost afraid to look. He opened the hospital file first.

They found semen from two men. Neither matched anything on file. They were probably related. The fetus was fathered by one of those men, which meant she had been with him for at least three months. The blood on her hands matched the other man. Maybe she'd injured him as she escaped.

Jake closed the folder and traded it for the one on the van. All the fingerprints matched the woman's. The blood in the back was also hers as well as the hair. The van may have been stolen with the intent of kidnapping her. Maybe she'd been tied up and tossed into the back.

Jake picked up the last one. It was a report on the dress. Short black hairs matched one semen sample. Longer blond hairs matched the other semen sample.

The label in the dress was from a high-end clothing designer. She might have purchased it new or from a second hand shop.

Chances were high that two men had kidnapped Jane Doe. Did they kidnap her to rape her or for ransom? If ransom, maybe the deal had fallen through and they'd taken it out on her. Jake was sure that if she hadn't escaped they would have killed her.

She hadn't given up and had found a way to escape. Many women are given a means of escape from their abusers, but don't. His heart swelled with pride for this woman whose voice he'd never heard and eyes he'd never seen.

Chapter 4

Jake's feet almost dragged as he walked into Jane Doe's room at seven o'clock. He hadn't had dinner yet, but he needed to see her first. Her hand was familiar in his now. "Hi, sunshine. It's Jake. I just found out today what a brave woman you are. Whatever's happened, I know you can face it and come out the victor. It's time to wake up."

She squeezed his hand.

"That's it. You're doing great. Wake up for Jake." His voice grew excited.

A whisper. "Jake?" Her eyes remained closed.

Jake crouched closer to her. "Sunshine, can you open your eyes for me?" Her eyelids fluttered like they were too heavy to lift. Finally, they opened and she stared at him. Her eyes were golden brown and beautiful. Her hand trembled in his.

"I bet you're real thirsty." He picked up a cup with a straw from her tray. "Do you want a drink?"

Her eyes didn't leave his as she nodded. He brought the straw to her mouth and she drank greedily, keeping her eyes on his. She released the straw and closed her eyes.

"Please don't go back to sleep yet."

Her eyelids fluttered and remained open.

"Can you tell me your name?"

"Sam."

"Ah, good. It's nice to meet you, Sam. I'm Jake. What's your last name?"

Sam's eyes widened and darted around the room then

16

focused on him. "I don't know." Her breath quickened.

"Calm down. It's okay. You've been in a coma for a week. You're bound to have some problems at first. What *do* you remember?"

She took some deep breaths and squinted. "My name is Sam. And your voice."

Sam gripped Jake's hand so tightly he'd have to pry each finger off. He pulled out his cell phone and dialed the hospital switchboard. "Can you page or call Dr. Alan Caldwell and Dr. Stacey Reynolds and have them call me at this number?" He rattled it off. Then he pressed the nurse's call button.

He turned back to the woman. "Sam, would you mind if I call you Sammie? Sam seems too masculine for you."

Sam pressed her other hand to her chest.

"Sam, are you okay?"

"Yeah. It's just that—my heart skipped a beat when you asked."

"So, I shouldn't call you Sammie?"

"I would like you to call me Sammie."

Jake's phone rang as a nurse, Beth, rushed in. She talked quietly with Sam as she took her vitals.

Sam's hand released him and he stepped away. "Dr. Caldwell."

"Sheriff, is there a problem?"

"No, Doctor. Our Jane Doe, no, Sam Doe woke up."

"Sam Doe?"

"Yeah. The only thing she remembers is that her first name is Sam."

"I'll call Dr. Reynolds."

"I've already put a call in to her."

"All right. I'll be in to check her out soon."

Jake slipped his phone into his pocket.

He stepped back to the bed and Sam held her hand out.

He dragged the chair closer, took her hand, and sat down next to her.

"Sammie, let me tell you about where you are." He waved his hand around. "This is a hospital."

She laughed and slapped his hand with her free one.

He smiled. "You're in Arkansas in a little community called Willow Ridge. The only reason we have a hospital is because it's in the center of the county. We've got more farm and ranch animals than people."

"And you're the sheriff?"

"That's me. Sheriff Jake Hamilton. But you can call me Jake." He smiled at her.

She smiled back. "I like you, Jake." Her voice grew quieter. "Thank you for talking to me. I think, at first, I didn't want to wake up." Tears glistened in her eyes. "Why would I feel that way?"

Her pain and confusion tightened his chest like a vise squeezing his heart. "It doesn't matter. From now on, you're going to look forward to each day and race to see what it has to offer you."

"Okay. I'll take your word for that." One corner of her mouth tipped up.

Jake's phone rang again. He fished it out of his pocket and answered. "Hi, Dr. Reynolds. This is Sheriff Hamilton. Can you come visit your newest patient tonight?"

"She's awake?"

"Yes. Just a few minutes ago. She seems to have amnesia."

"I should be there in a half-hour or so."

"Thanks. I'll see you soon."

"Who is Dr. Reynolds?"

"She's a psychologist who—mostly has women patients." She didn't need to know that Dr. Reynolds had mostly battered women as patients.

Jake told Sam funny stories about being a sheriff in a small community.

They were chuckling when a short woman with curly black hair entered the room.

"Dr. Reynolds?" At her nod, Jake freed his hand and got up. "Can we talk in the hall for a minute?"

She turned around and headed out the door.

Jake pulled the door closed behind him. "She says the only thing she can remember is that her name is Sam. I kind of wish she didn't have to dredge up the trauma she's been through, that she could start fresh with new memories, but I'd also like to know who did this to her so we can put them away."

"We'll go at her pace. She'll remember when she's ready to. Maybe it'll only be bits and pieces or maybe it will all rush back to her. She seems to have a pretty disturbing history, so I'm not going to force anything. We'll take it slow."

"That's reassuring. I'm going to go say goodnight and leave her to you."

Jake went back into the room and took Sam's hand. "Sammie, I have to go. I'll come back in the morning. Dr. Reynolds wants to talk to you now."

Her hand trembled in his and her eyes widened, like he'd seen on so many domestic calls. "It's all right. I wouldn't leave you with her if I didn't trust her. Will you be okay?"

She squeezed his hand and wouldn't let go. "Jake, you're the only person I know." She darted a look to Dr. Reynolds.

The doctor stepped closer to Sam and rested her hand on the rail. In a gentle, calming voice she said, "Sam, call me Stacey. I'm just here to help you deal with this problem you're having."

Sam released her death trip on Jake's hand, but didn't let

go. "I'm afraid and I don't know why."

Stacey nodded. "We're going to see what we can do about that. Why don't you let the sheriff leave and we'll have some girl talk."

Sam gazed at Jake.

He covered her hand with his free one. "Sam, Dr. Reynolds wants to help you."

She slowly nodded. "Will I see you tomorrow?"

"Of course. I'll stop in before I go to the office."

"Thank you." She released him.

If Dr. Reynolds hadn't been there, he would have been tempted to kiss Sam on the forehead. He didn't know how he'd gotten so attached to a woman who'd only opened her eyes a couple of hours ago.

On the way down the hall, he left a quick message for Alex that the woman was awake, but would be no help yet because she had amnesia.

Chapter 5

Jake entered Sam's room in the morning, happy to see her eating breakfast. She was so thin. He wondered if she was normally thin or if her treatment over the last few months caused it.

"Sammie, it's so good to see you awake." He took a seat on a chair next to her.

She smiled and held her hand out to him. "I need to hold your hand." Her eyes pleaded. "It's still the only thing I can remember, your voice and your hand holding mine."

Jake took Sammie's hand. It was right where it belonged. He didn't know how he'd come up with so many things to say to her when she was unconscious and unable to respond. But somehow his one-sided conversations, hand-holding and watching over her had made him feel close to her.

"Dr. Caldwell came in this morning," Sam said.

"And what did he have to say?"

"He checked me out and asked if I was having any pain."

"Are you?" Jake asked with concern.

"Not much. My head hurts a little and my ribs are a bit achy. Um, Jake?"

He squeezed her hand tighter. She bit her lip and her eyes dropped to their joined hands.

"What is it, sunshine?"

"When I talked to Stacey last night, she said she'd help me to remember. But I had this awful feeling." Tears

21

glistened in her eyes. "I don't think I want to remember."

He scooted to the edge of his chair, and touched her cheek. "You don't have to if you're not ready for it. Dr. Reynolds said she would let you go at your own pace. Maybe that means you're at a standstill for a while."

She covered the hand on her cheek. Her shoulders dropped. "Thank you."

Jake pulled his hand away. "Now finish your breakfast."

They talked until she was done. "I've got to get to the station." He stood and when he reached toward her to take her hand he felt an object in his coat pocket. "Oh, I almost forgot. I brought you a book from home. Michael Crichton, *Sphere*. I thought you might get bored today." He handed it to her. "He's one of my favorite authors."

Sam took it from him. "Thank you. The name sounds familiar, but I don't even know if I like him. I guess I'll find out." She smiled.

~~~

Sam turned the page of the book then glanced up when she heard a footstep. The man wore scrubs and had a stethoscope around his neck. His dark eyes matched his hair and his smile revealed his dimples.

"Stop! Who are you?"

He paused. "I'm one of the nurses on duty, Wade Stuart. I just need to check your vitals."

Her hands trembled, she gripped the book tighter in hopes it would make them stop. It didn't help. This man meant to hurt her. She didn't know why she knew that, but she did.

He took two more steps.

She raised her voice. "I said, stop!"

He held up his hands. His dimples were gone, replaced

with a wrinkle between his brows. "It's all right. I'm not going to hurt you. I've been in here before."

"Not that I'm aware of. Get out or I'll scream." She wanted to cry but she had to be strong. She wasn't tied up, so she could run if she needed to. Fear twisted in her gut at the thought of being tied up.

"I'm leaving. I'll have another nurse check you."

He backed out of the room and she fell back against the pillow, her shoulders sag. She didn't understand what just happened. It was ridiculous to think the nurse would hurt her. He left when she told him to, so that must mean she was wrong.

With still shaking hands, she set her book on the tray table and clasped her hands together. She blinked and a tear slid down her cheek. Maybe she wasn't so strong after all.

A nurse came in. She thought her name was Liz and was relieved when she read the name tag. At least some things stayed in her memory.

"Sam, what's wrong? Wade said you made him leave."

She shook her head. "I don't know. He scared me."

Liz chuckled. "I'll have to tease him about that. He doesn't usually get that reaction from the lady patients. Let me check your vitals."

In a few minutes she'd taken Sam's blood pressure, listened to her heart and checked her eyes.

"Hmm. Your blood pressure is a little higher than usual, but it's probably from the scare."

Sam nodded. Her gaze kept returning to the door, afraid Wade would come back.

Liz must have read her mind. She patted her arm. "I'll make sure that only female nurses check on you."

"Thank you. I don't mean to be trouble."

"It's all right, dear." She tipped her head. "You don't have a problem with Dr. Caldwell."

"No. He's really kind." But, she hadn't given Wade a chance to show if he was kind or not.

"And then there's the scrumptious sheriff."

She grinned. "He's even better than kind." She hadn't thought about Jake being scrumptious. He was the person she was most comfortable with and even then it was sometimes too much. She felt safest when she was totally alone, which didn't happen often enough. Except being alone the night before was just as bad as when they checked on her.

She took a deep breath. "I'm okay now." Maybe that would get Liz to leave and she could be alone and safe again.

~~~

The next morning as Jake got out of his car at the hospital, he touched his pocket to reassure himself that he had remembered to grab another book before he left home. He'd enjoyed his visit with Sam the night before. She'd gotten about two-thirds through the book he'd given her, and they'd had a fun discussion about it. He realized again how smart Sam was. She picked apart some scenes in the story, but backed up her thoughts with sound reasoning. He was amazed at the details she'd noticed that he'd missed. She still loved the book, though.

He strolled through Sam's door. "Morning, sunshine." Sam's face lit up with such a brilliant smile, his gut tensed. Something about her wrapped itself around him.

"Jake, the best times of my day are when you're here."

He smiled as he pulled out the book.

"Another one? I can't wait." Sam clapped her hands together. "I'm going to finish this one this morning." She rested her hand on the book on her table.

They talked for a while before Jake told Sam he had to leave.

Her face stilled. "But you'll come tonight?"

"I wouldn't miss it." He leaned forward and stopped himself. What was he thinking? He almost gave her a kiss on the forehead. After what she'd been through, it would have been the worst thing to do. Instead he touched her hand.

"Have a good day, Jake." Sam gave him a small smile.

He stopped at the nurses' station. "Liz, is Dr. Caldwell on the floor?"

The nurse pointed down the hall in the opposite direction from Sam's room. "He's down that way, Sheriff. He should be out any minute."

Jake walked in that direction and the doctor stepped out of a room almost in front of him.

"Morning, Doctor."

"Good Morning, Sheriff. What can I do for you?"

"Can you tell me how Sam is doing?"

Dr. Caldwell gave a questioning expression. "She had a good day yesterday, except for the incident with the male nurse.

Jake's brows came down. "What did he do?"

"He went to her room to take vitals. She threatened to scream if he didn't leave."

"What did he do to her?"

The doctor shook his head. "He didn't get near her. He left and sent in another nurse. Her blood pressure was a little high, but that's to be expected with a scare."

"Can I talk to this nurse?"

"Of course. Just ask for Wade at the nurse's station."

"Thanks. So, other than that, she's all right?"

"Yes. Barring any unexpected issues today, I want to release her tomorrow morning. I've contacted the women's shelter and asked if they can take her in."

"What? The shelter? I can't imagine that being a good option for her. She's not ready to see those battered women."

"You may be right, Sheriff, but what other option is there?"

"She'll come home with me," Jake said firmly. The words were out before his brain had even registered them.

The doctor's voice rose. "What? I don't think so."

Jake's mind raced. The more he thought about it, the more he liked the idea. "I own a ranch. I have a live-in housekeeper so Sam would have constant female company."

Dr. Caldwell's expression reminded Jake of a man who'd been lied to too many times.

"I'll call Dr. Reynolds about it," Jake said.

"Yeah, you do that." The doctor entered another patient's room.

Jake went in search of Wade. He didn't learn anything useful. The man couldn't have been involved in Sammie's kidnapping. He was on duty fifty hours a week and hadn't had a vacation in almost a year. Maybe he looked something like one of the men who hurt her or maybe he startled her. He'd still have Alex get a swab from him and compare it to the DNA samples.

~~~

The first thing Jake did when he got into his office was check the missing person reports. He figured there was only a slim chance that Sam would be reported missing after she'd been gone for as much as three months, but he didn't have any real options for finding out her identity. He'd thought it would be cleared up when she woke from the coma.

The next thing he did was call Dr. Reynolds' office. He was surprised when she answered his call instead of a receptionist.

"Hi, Doctor. This is Sheriff Hamilton. How did your visit with Sam go yesterday?"

"Now, Sheriff, you know I can't discuss that with you."

"I was afraid of that." He took a breath. "The reason for my call is that Dr. Caldwell told me this morning that he'll probably release Sam tomorrow. He said he's releasing her to the women's shelter. I don't think that would be good for her."

"I agree with you. The exposure to all those women in emotional or physical pain would probably put her into a tailspin."

"Sam can come home with me."

The doctor raised her voice. "Absolutely not!"

"Hear me out. It's not like I live in a bachelor pad. I own a ranch outside of town. I have a huge house and a live-in housekeeper. Sam can have as much space as she needs and Abby, my housekeeper can look out for her."

"That does have possibilities. Why do you want to do this?"

He let out his breath. "I'm the one who found her. I sat with her while we waited for the ambulance to come. I've been checking up on her. I just somehow feel a connection with her. She doesn't deserve to have anything else bad happen to her."

"Let me think about it. I'll let you know later today. Oh, can you give me your house number? I'd like to talk to your housekeeper."

Chapter 6

When Jake entered Sam's room that evening, her grin reached ear to ear. "Jake, I'm being released tomorrow. When Dr. Caldwell told me, I panicked. Where would I go? Then Stacey came and talked to me. She told me that you offered your house. She talked to your housekeeper, and she's pretty confident that it's a good place for me. Thank you so much."

"So, you're accepting?" Dr. Reynolds had approved. She hadn't told him. Jake was relieved, he couldn't imagine her going to the women's shelter. He knew Sam had gotten comfortable with him but wasn't sure if it was enough to actually move into his house.

She held her hand out to him. He rushed to her and took it in his.

"Yes, I'm accepting. I can't wait to get out of—" A frown overtook her happy expression.

"Sammie, what's wrong?"

"I- don't have any clothes. I can't waltz out of here like this." She pulled at the neck of her hospital gown.

"Ah, I see your point." His eyes crinkled with a smile. "How about if I ask Abby, my housekeeper, to pick up everything you need in the morning and bring it all here?"

Her eyes flashed her surprise. "I can't ask you to do that. I don't have any way to repay you."

"The alternative is for you to live day and night in that pretty gown." Jake chuckled.

Her eyes widened and then she smiled. "You're right.

Thank you."

He sat down and they talked for a while. Finally, he said, "I've got to go. Tomorrow I'll find out what time you're being discharged and I'll come by then."

"Okay. Thanks again, Jake."

As he left the building, he hoped he was doing the right thing. He knew Sam couldn't go to the women's shelter. It would traumatize her. There was nowhere else she could go. Most of all, he wanted to keep her safe. They didn't know what had happened to her. She could still be in danger.

~~~

Sam turned the page of her book and glanced up when someone tapped on her door. Doctors, nurses and staff would just push the door open and walk in and her only visitors were Jake and Stacey.

"Come in."

A pretty woman, probably around thirty pushed the door open and stepped in. Her dark hair was in a short braid. She wore jeans, a red plaid shirt and boots. "I'm Abby." She stopped beside Sam's bed.

"Jake's housekeeper."

She set a plastic bag on the bed and opened it. "I figured it would be a good idea to get an idea what size clothes you needed before I bought any." She shook her head. "Men aren't any good at that."

She pulled out a shirt, pants, panties and bra. "I thought you could try these on and we could more easily guess sizes."

Sam smiled. "That sounds great."

She slid her feet out of the bed and stood. Picking up the clothes, she gathered the back of her hospital gown closed and went into the bathroom. She had no idea what size she wore, but at least she knew how to put on the clothes and button the shirt.

Sam stepped back out. Abby jumped up from the chair beside the bed. "That doesn't look too bad. You're close to my size."

Abby pulled a small spiral pad and pen from her purse and took notes on their decisions on sizes.

Sam turned. "I'll be right back." In the bathroom, she changed back into the gown and folded the clothes. Returning to her room, she handed them to Abby and sat on the edge of her bed.

"Thanks."

As Abby pushed the clothes back into the bag. "I'll get toiletries, too."

Sam stared at her clenched hands and then at Abby's face. "So, do you like working for Jake?" That might be a good indication of how it would be to live in his house. She thought she could trust him, but she was still going to a stranger's house in the middle of nowhere.

Abby looked Sam in the eye. "He's a good man. He was the officer who came when my neighbors called in that my husband was beating me."

Sam gasped and tears sprung to her eyes. It felt like she'd heard this story before, but it slipped away before she could grasp it.

Abby held up a hand. "It's okay. Jake took him down and cuffed him. It's the most angry I've ever seen Jake. He called for backup to take him away. Then Jake took me to the hospital. I was there for two days. I was going to end up at the women's shelter, but Jake offered me a place on the ranch."

Abby picked up her bag and smiled. "It's been the best two years of my life."

Sam frowned. "And you're the only woman there?"

Abby patted Sam's hand. "They're all great guys. Paul, the foreman, makes sure everybody stays in line."

Sam noticed the sparkle in Abby's eyes when she said Paul's name. It made her feel more comfortable going to a ranch full of men, even though she didn't know why she felt uncomfortable to begin with.

~~~

It was almost noon when Jake stepped into Sam's room. She was dressed and sitting on a chair beside her bed. He grinned and she gave him a tentative smile. Jake squatted in front of her. "Hey, sunshine, are you okay?"

She nodded. "I'm a little nervous. Not that it's much of a home, but the hospital is the only place I know."

"You'll be fine. Since you're not wearing that attractive hospital gown anymore, I assume Abby stopped by with clothes for you."

"Yes, thank you. She called to ask me for sizes but I didn't know. So, she stopped here before shopping. Fortunately, we're nearly the same size, so she figured it out. I couldn't believe all the stuff she brought back for me."

"Hmm." He frowned. "She's trying to bankrupt me again." At her worried look, Jake laughed. "I'm teasing."

She smiled. "We went through the clothes and I picked out what to wear today, then Abby said she'd take everything else—home for me."

She took his hand. "I really like her. I'm glad I got to meet her before going to your house."

He stood and pulled her up. It was the first time that they'd actually stood next to each other. She was shorter than he expected. Probably shorter than any woman he'd dated. He reminded himself that they weren't dating. What Sammie needed right now was a friend and a safe place to recover.

For just a second fear filled her eyes. Maybe she was also thinking about how much bigger he was than her. He took a step back. She blinked then smiled.

Outside, he helped her climb into his truck. "Sorry. I forgot that you might have trouble with this. I just figured you'd be more comfortable riding in my truck than in the cruiser."

"It's okay. I'm up here now and you're right. This is better than riding in your cruiser."

Jake drove through town, smiling at how avidly Sam looked at everything and slowed down. She was glowing like a kid at Christmas time. How blank was her mind?

"Have you ever been to a small town like this before?"

~~~

Sam didn't answer immediately. "I don't think so. I had a flash of tall buildings."

It seemed so strange. Each thing she saw was a new memory to fill the void in her head. She knew she lived in the United States. She had a pretty good knowledge of the country's history, but it still bothered her that she didn't even know who the president was. At least she knew there *was* a president.

She continued watching everything that past the window. They rode through what was probably the center of town. Cars lined the street and there were many small shops. There was a restaurant with its own parking lot beside it that was nearly full. It reminded her that she hadn't had lunch yet. Her stomach growled and she covered it with her hand.

Jake chuckled. "Lunch is waiting at the ranch."

Stores gave way to mostly one story neatly maintained houses. After a few blocks, there was a good size grocery store and a discount department store beside it.

They reached the edge of town and he sped up. After that there were miles of empty fields. The truck slowed as it came to a sharp curve. She felt his eyes on her, turned and smiled. She wasn't sure what the look he gave her meant. In twenty minutes they were pulling into a driveway with a sign over it that read *Twin Creeks Ranch*.

"Is this your place?"

"Yep. My grandfather bought the land. And it actually *is* bordered on two sides by creeks."

It must have been a half mile before they reached a white two story house with lots of windows and a covered porch across the front. He stopped near the porch, jumped out and hurried to the other side of the truck and opened the door.

Sam stared at the barn that was about a hundred feet from the house. It was a traditional red with a barn style roof. Attached to the side of it was a paddock surrounded by a split rail fence. Two horses grazed inside. Her shoulders dropped, tension easing out of them. For the first time since she woke from the coma she felt safe.

"You ready, Sammie?"

Her heart skipped a beat and she bit her bottom lip, but nodded. Her arm tensed when he put his hand around it to help her down. She side-stepped away from him before he led her to the house.

They stepped inside and he waved his arm. "Welcome to my home. I hope you'll feel safe here."

They stood in a big entry area. To the right was an impersonal living room, very neat. It was probably only used for company. The stairs were beside it. Straight ahead was a wide hallway and to her left a more comfortable looking family room. There was a wide screen TV on the wall with lots of couches and chairs facing it.

She smiled. "Thank you. I do already." It seemed

strange he said safe instead of comfortable. Was there something or someone she should fear? Maybe that's why her mind was blank. She was afraid of something and didn't want to remember it.

"Ah, let me show you to your room." He headed to the stairs and she followed. "This first room is mine." He pointed to the left. He past two more doors and turned to the right. "This is your room."

She followed him in and immediately felt at home. The walls were a pale blue. The curtains and bedspread a darker blue. The hardwood floor gleamed. "It's so nice and sunny. It's beautiful." The only place she recalled living was the hospital, so almost anything would be better.

Jake pointed to the left. "That's the closet and beside it is the bathroom. I see Abby left your clothes on the bed. Do you want to put them away now or after lunch?"

"Oh, definitely after lunch." Her stomach growled to emphasize her choice.

Chuckling, he led her back downstairs and to the back of the house.

Pans clattered as they entered the kitchen. "Hey, Abby. Thanks for shopping this morning. What's for lunch?"

Abby turned. "Hi, Jake. Hi, Sam. Vegetable beef soup and sandwiches. Help yourselves. The hands have been in already, so you've got the dining room to yourselves."

Jake ladled soup into a bowl from the stack beside the pan. He handed it to Sam. He ladled a bowl for himself and led her to the dining table. A stack of sandwiches sat under a clear lid with plates sitting beside it. Cups held spoons, forks and knives.

"Sammie, have a seat. Would you like milk, ice tea, lemonade, water or soda?"

"Water is fine. Thanks."

He returned with their drinks and sat down opposite her.

"Usually all six ranch hands are here for breakfast and one to six for lunch, depending on what work they're doing. They're usually all here for dinner. I know you might not be comfortable with a bunch of strange guys at first, so feel free to have your meals in my office. I have a small table in there."

She caught her bottom lip with her teeth. The thought of a bunch of big men scared her and she didn't know why. Maybe she'd always been fearful. "Thanks. I guess I'll wait to see how I feel." At least she'd try to show a brave front.

As they ate, he told her about the ranch. At the mention of horses, excitement filled her.

"Do you ride?"

"I don't know, but I'd love to see the horses."

"After I show you around the house, we'll go out to the barn. In a few days I'll take you out for a ride, and we'll see how you do."

"That sounds wonderful." She smiled.

When they finished eating, Jake picked up his dishes and took them to the kitchen. Sam picked up hers and followed.

He pointed. "Back there is Abby's space. She's got a bedroom, living room and bathroom. He went towards the front of the house and stepped through a doorway they previously past. "This is my office. He pointed to an over full bookcase. "You can take whatever books you want to read. If you want romances, I know Abby has some that she can loan you."

She wandered to a window with a table before it. "Oh, wow. The cows are so close."

Jake chuckled. "We call them cattle."

"Oh, sorry."

"Let me show you the rest."

Once they finished in the house, Jake took Sam to the barn. They walked between empty stalls and he stopped in front of one with a horse. "This is Saffron. She's been sick so we're keeping her away from the others."

"Is she going to be okay?"

"Yeah, she's on the mend." He rubbed the horse's nose. "You're doing lots better, huh, Saffron?"

"Can I touch her?" She was itching to feel the warm animal.

"She'd enjoy that."

Sam carefully touched Saffron's nose. She flattened her fingers and rubbed down. "She feels so—alive." She talked to the horse for a few minutes. It felt familiar.

"Let's go outside and you can meet the horses in the paddock. We let out the ones we aren't using for work."

"You actually ride the range on horses?"

"We've got a couple of pick-ups, too. Whatever works."

Three horses stood in the paddock, one eating grass. Jake whistled and their ears perked up. He called out, "Smoky!" The dark gray horse trotted over.

"Whoa! He's a lot bigger than Saffron." Sam took a step back from the fence.

Jake reached up to Smoky's halter and talked quietly to him. "He's okay, Sammie. Look, he's curious about you."

Sam stepped to the fence and slowly raised her hand up to the side of the horse's neck. "Hi, Smoky. You're a pretty boy, aren't you?" The horse stared at her with one big eye then stretched his neck and took Sam by surprise when he nibbled her neck with his lips.

She laughed and stepped back. "That tickles."

Jake laughed, too. "I've never seen him do that before. I think you have an admirer."

She reached up to the horse again. "Smoky, are you my friend? My second friend?"

Chapter 7

Sam sat in a chair near the window in her room, reading, looking out whenever movement caught her eye. The horses grazed around the paddock. Men walked to or from the barn. A black pickup drove up, someone loaded tools into it and drove across the field. Several hours later, it came back and the workers unloaded the tools.

The chair was cozy. The sunlight through the window warmed her. The room was comfortable and made her feel safe. Safe. It seemed to be a word she thought about a lot and didn't know why. And she didn't want to know why.

A knock on the door brought her out of her book with a start. She clutched the book to her chest, afraid of the pain she'd feel when the door opened. Her gaze swept the room and she gulped in deep breaths until she remembered she was at Jake's house. She didn't know why fear would paralyzed her. The knock came again, and setting her book down, she walked across the room and with a trembling hand, opened the door. Jake stood in front of her and she sagged against the doorframe as relief washed over her.

He wrinkled his brow before speaking, so he must have seen her reaction.

"I thought I would escort you down to dinner and introduce you to the ranch hands."

Her hand tightened on the door and her heart, which had started to calm, raced again.

His next words calmed her somewhat.

"We won't linger. I just want you to be familiar with

their names and faces. Then we'll eat in my office. Do you think you can do that?"

Sam nodded but her shoulders tensed. This fear was unexpected. When they reached the bottom of the stairs, the voices of men in the kitchen drifted to them. She slowed then stopped. It sounded like a lot of voices. The men she'd seen through the window had been big, probably strong from carrying all kinds of heavy stuff. They could hurt her so easily. Her stomach knotted up and she placed her fist over it. She'd been hungry upstairs, but now if she ate, she didn't think the food would stay down.

Jake waited near the dining room doorway. "It's okay. It'll only take a couple of minutes."

She looked into Jake's eyes. He'd saved her. He wouldn't let anything happen to her. She nodded again and took a tentative step. *You can do this.* She didn't know why she was so afraid of those men. Even hearing their voices caused her heart to race. Jake would stay with her so it would be fine. There was no reason why it wouldn't be fine.

When they stepped into the kitchen all talking stopped. All eyes were on her. *I'm sure they see I'm afraid. Why am I afraid of them?*

"Hi, guys," Jake said cheerfully. "I'd like you to meet Sam. She's going to stay with us for a little while. Sam, this is Paul, my foreman." He was the tallest of the group.

Paul nodded. "Evenin', Ma'am."

Jake pointed to each one as he said his name. "Adam, Steve, Hugo, Tim and Andy." Each nodded in turn.

"It's nice to meet you." She could barely get the words out. She hoped they'd heard her. And hoped she didn't look as scared as she felt.

Jake picked up two plates from the table. "Sam and I are eating in my office tonight, so we'll fill our plates and get out of the way." He'd mostly said it to reassure Sammie that they weren't staying. Within a couple of minutes they walked into Jake's office and set their food on a small square table near the window. Jake pulled out a chair for her to sit and then sat opposite her.

She took a deep breath to calm herself. She'd done it. Nothing bad had happened, but Jake had been there.

While they ate, Jake talked about the history of his ranch. How his grandfather bought it and kept buying more pieces. How he kept increasing the size of his herd. "I've mostly been maintaining. It's been thirty years since the size of the ranch has increased."

"How big is it?"

"Two-hundred-fifty acres. The size of our herd fluctuates depending on weather and the economy."

They talked well after they'd finished eating. After her third yawn, Jake shook his head. "Sammie, I forgot this is your first day out of the hospital. It looks like you should call it a night."

She yawned again and laughed. "You're right. I'm exhausted."

They gathered their plates, and she followed him to the kitchen. It was empty. After putting their dishes in the sink, Jake touched Sam's arm. When she tensed, he quickly removed it.

"Now off with you. Maybe I'll see you in the morning before I leave."

~~~

After Sam disappeared around a corner, Jake swore. He shouldn't have touched her. It happened before he even knew what he was doing. He'd felt her reaction. He'd frightened her and he didn't want to ever do that. He headed out to the bunkhouse.

When he stepped through the door of the main room, the guys stopped talking. "Hey, what's up, boss?" Tim asked.

"I just wanted to let you know that you have to treat Sam very carefully. She has amnesia and she's real skittish around men. We don't know yet what's happened to her. Remember how Abby was when she first came?"

All but Adam nodded. He hadn't been there when Abby first arrived.

Sam looked directly at Adam. "You were here when Fawn arrived?"

Adam nodded.

"I remember seeing you spend a lot of time talking to her, working your way closer until you got her to eat from your hand."

Adam nodded. "Yeah. It was tough. Her previous owner treated her bad. It took months to get her to trust us. Now she's one of our best horses."

Jake smiled. "Exactly. So, same with Sam. No sudden moves, let her be the one to approach you and be careful what you say."

They all chorused their understanding.

"Thanks, guys."

Chapter 8

As they ate breakfast in Jake's office on Sam's fourth day in his house, she tried to encourage herself to actually talk to one of the ranch hands.

She was getting to know Abby by helping her prepare meals, but she still took her food to Jake's office before the men came in. When she knew all the men were out, she would sneak out to the barn and visit with the horses. The rest of the time, she was either in her room or Jake's office, curled up in a chair, reading. That was where she was the most comfortable. She discovered that she enjoyed Jake's sci-fi books and the medical thrillers as well as Abby's romance novels.

Looking up from her plate, she saw a gleam in Jake's eye.

"How would you like to go for a ride this morning?"

Sam's eyes widened. "Ride? As in horseback ride?"

He nodded.

She jumped out of her chair, raced to the other side of the table and threw her arms around Jake's neck and immediately released him, stepping back. Her hand flew over her open mouth.

"Umm. Sorry. Yes?" She was shocked at what she'd done. She'd reacted to the joy of having a ride and then it hit her and for just a second she was scared. She shouldn't have touched him. The fear receded when Jake laughed.

"Yeah, I did understand that to mean 'yes'."

She blushed.

Jake gestured at her clothes. "Those jeans are fine, but you should probably put on a long-sleeved shirt. That pale skin can burn pretty fast. Your sneakers will have to do since you don't have boots."

"Just give me two minutes." She held up two fingers then turned and rushed off.

The horses waited outside the barn when she returned. Jake slid a rifle into the saddle and turned. She stopped and stared at it.

"A gun?" It frightened her. Jake was the sheriff and carried a handgun. Something about this felt different.

He pointed over his shoulder. "We never go out there without one. We might run into a coyote or a cattle rustler or a hundred other dangers."

She bit her lip and nodded. It made sense. It was to keep them safe. So, why didn't the gun make her feel safe?

She shook off the feeling and smiled. "Saffron and Smoky." They were her two favorite horses.

"You remembered."

"I've been visiting them and it's not like I've got a huge amount of information in my head that would crowd it out."

Jake turned quickly to Sam and frowned. "Are you okay?"

She nodded. "Mostly. I know there are things I don't want to remember, but it would be nice to remember some of the little things. Like, do I ride a horse? What do I like on pizza? At least I know what pizza is." And so many more, like, did she have a husband, boyfriend, kids even? Was there other family? If so, why was no one trying to find her? Jake didn't discuss it with her, but she knew he must be looking.

He wrinkled his brow. "I'm sorry that this is frustrating for you. But you *are* making new memories that can help fill in that empty space." He tapped his forehead.

He circled the horse and patted the other one. "You'll ride Saffron. She's gentle and itching to get out. It'll be her first outing since she's been sick. My usual mount is Smoky."

He helped her into the saddle and explained how to hold the reins and give the horse instruction. Then he mounted the gray horse and smiled at her.

"You okay?"

"I'm good," She tried not to smile, but it escaped anyway. This was the most excited she'd felt since she woke from the coma.

They started out at a walk. Jake gave her some pointers and increased their pace. She wanted to see everything. The land was fairly flat, so miles of grass and bushes stretched around her. The grass beneath the horses was closely cropped. She remembered that on her first day on the ranch, cattle were closer to the house and guessed that they'd been moved to an area with taller grass. To their left, a row of trees about a mile away blocked her view.

She pointed. "Are those trees intentionally planted like that?"

"Yes, they're a windbreak. With so much open space they're needed to protect the land from erosion and they help reduce snow drifting. On some of the hotter days the cattle congregate in the shadows."

~~~

Jake was surprised she rode as well as he did. "Are you ready to go faster?" At her nod, he explained how to increase speed. They went at a nice canter for a little while until she slowed down.

It was only then that he noticed how hard she was breathing. "I'm sorry. I forgot you just got out of the hospital. I don't want to overtax you."

Between heavy breaths she struggled to speak. "That's okay. It was fun. Slow for a bit will be good, though."

If Sammie had been tied up for the last few months, no wonder she was so out of shape.

"There's a canteen hanging from your saddle with water, if you're thirsty."

She picked it up and took a long drink. "Ah. Delicious."

After riding at the slower pace for several minutes, she kicked Saffron into a slow jog and he increased his speed to keep up.

He could barely keep his eyes off her. The warm sun shining on her hair turned the tips golden as the wind blew it behind her. He kept pace beside her. After a little while she slowed to a walk again.

He pointed a half mile ahead of them to a lone tree. "Let's head over to that tree." When they arrived, Jake got off Smoky and helped her down then led the horses under the tree. He removed a blanket from his saddle bag and spread it out in the shade. "Have a seat."

He went back to his horse and pulled out a bag and his canteen. When he turned back, Sam had pulled half the blanket into the sun and was sitting on the sunny half. He sat on the blanket beside her and opened his bag, pulling out packages of sliced cheddar cheese and sliced apples. "You ready for a snack?"

"That sounds wonderful. I can't believe how hungry I am." She reached for a piece of cheese. "Jake, I think I know how to ride. At first I was a little uncomfortable, but the longer I was in the saddle, the more my body automatically took over."

"I agree. You picked up Saffron's rhythm really quickly and I didn't have to remind you what to do. You even did a couple of things without my even mentioning it."

They ate some more and Sam had another drink. Then she lay back on the blanket and closed her eyes. "The sun feels so nice. I've been really enjoying it the past few days. It's almost like I've been in the dark for weeks." She shivered.

"You okay, Sammie?" He wanted to touch her but held back.

"Yeah." She opened her eyes. "It's— What's that phrase? It felt like someone walked over my grave?" She shivered again, fright in her eyes.

He was glad that her eyes were closed again so that she didn't see *him* shiver. If what he suspected was true, she'd been days from death.

He stretched out on the blanket beside her. He'd just watch her while he waited for her to be ready to go back.

Jake woke up, opened his eyes and tipped his hand to glance at his watch. He'd been asleep about an hour. Her face was slightly pink from too much sun. He was surprised she'd curled up with her head against his side. His arm ran along her back. It was the perfect way to wake up, but he wasn't sure how she would respond. He didn't want to wake her by moving, but didn't want her to wake up and be frightened. He was still debating when she stirred. He'd have to hope for the best.

Sam opened her eyes and then stilled, not even breathing. She jerked to a sitting position with fear in her eyes, her sun flushed cheeks paled. She turned her head from side to side, inspecting everything around her and put her hand over her ear, closed her eyes for a second. "Oh, Jake! I'm so glad it's you. I had this awful feeling for a moment." She blinked several times and by the glisten in her eyes, he knew she was trying not to cry.

"Sorry, Sammie. I fell asleep, too and when I woke, I found you snuggled against me."

"I-I guess I'm comfortable with you." She stared at her entwined hands.

"That was one of the nicest things anyone's ever said to me." He cleared his throat. "Are you ready to go back now?"

Chapter 9

Two weeks later, while Sam and Jake were having breakfast, he said, "Sammie, we haven't been able to find any missing person report on you. I check every morning with no result."

Sam stared at him. "What does that mean?"

"It might mean we aren't checking the right part of the country. It could mean that there *is* no one to report you missing. Or that someone doesn't want to report you missing."

"So, I probably don't have anyone out there who cares about me?" She took a deep breath and tried to hide how sad it made her that she had no one.

Jake covered her hand. "I don't believe that. There's another reason that we just don't know yet. I'd like to release a picture of you to the networks in a couple of areas."

"No!" She jumped up, her breath coming in short bursts like she'd run a marathon. "They'll find me!" She panicked, looking around. If he did that, she'd have to hide.

Jake stood and gently took her stiff hands. "Who'll find you, Sammie?"

She stared at him for many seconds, finally frowned and asked, "Who?"

"You just said 'They'll find me.' Who will find you?"

She shook her head, puzzled. "I don't know. I don't remember saying that." Tears ran down her cheeks. What was happening to her? She forgot something that happened seconds ago.

Jake lightly held her arms as he pulled her toward him, then held her in his arms. Shivering, she wrapped her arms around his waist and held him. She held him tighter. She was safe. Jake would keep her safe. Why did she need to feel safe?

She finally loosened her hold and Jake pulled back, studying her tear stained face. "Are you okay?"

She pulled in a deep breath. "Yeah. I don't know what happened."

He touched her wet cheek. "Just remember, you're safe here."

She nodded. "I know. Thank you."

"I've got to get to work. Will you be all right?"

She nodded.

"Do you want me to have Abby take you for a ride today? She'll have one of the guys go with you. Even Abby doesn't ride alone."

She nodded and smiled. She'd be fine. Nothing had changed. "Okay. Thank you."

~~~

One of the first things Jake did after he sat down at his desk was call Dr. Reynolds. He explained to her what had happened that morning.

"That certainly sounds like a memory was trying to break through and Sam pushed it back. She doesn't feel ready to look at that part of her life yet."

"Yeah, I thought she was trying to protect herself."

"I'm glad you called me. I'm coming out this afternoon for our weekly session and this may have caused some changes for her."

~~~

By the time Jake pulled up to the house at dusk, he was ready to relax. It had been a long, tough day. A half day of school and a couple of teens with new drivers' licenses and too much free time, spelled disaster. They'd missed the same curve in the road that Sam had. Henry hadn't been able to determine how many times the car had rolled. At least they'd had their seatbelts on. One kid had a broken arm and the other a mild concussion. And they were both grounded according to their parents.

The highway department talked for years about rerouting the road, but nothing had come of it yet.

Jake rubbed his temples. Maybe a couple aspirin before dinner would help. He got out of the car and headed to the house. He met Sam at the bottom of the stairs.

"You look like you have a headache."

"It shows?" At her nod, he continued, "Yeah, it was a rough day. I was just going to get some aspirin."

"After you take them, why don't you meet me in your office and I'll massage your neck. Sometimes it helps....something." She shrugged and smiled. "These little snippets are so annoying."

A few minutes later Jake walked into his office. Sam jumped out of a chair. "I suggested the massage so quickly, that I must know how to do it, right? So have a seat." She pointed to the shorter backed chair in front of Jake's desk. "We'll see if I can do this."

He'd put on a t-shirt, so there wouldn't be a collar in the way. Sam stood behind him for a couple of seconds before touching him. She put a hand on each shoulder, squeezed with a little bit of pressure. She moved her hands toward Jake's neck and squeezed again. Tight muscles barely gave under her fingers. Then her hands seemed to remember what to do and moved just right.

He moaned as Sammie kneaded an especially tight kink

and it relaxed. Her magic hands massaged and relaxed muscles that must have been tense for months. Her fingers worked halfway down his spine, finding more tight muscles and treated them. He didn't think it could get any better until her fingers pushed through his hair and massaged his scalp. The first few strokes of her thumbs on the back of his skull intensified the pain, but his whole body melted after that.

Jake groaned.

She patted his shoulders. "There, how does that feel?"

Jake rolled his neck. "I can't believe how much that helped. My headache is almost gone." He smiled at her over his shoulder. "Thank you, Sammie. You made my night." At her blush, he continued, "What I mean is, that kind of headache usually lasts all evening and I can hardly feel it now."

He twisted and took her hands in his. "You knew how to do a massage. Do you think you're a massage therapist?

She bit her lip. "I don't know. I didn't even know why I asked you, but my hands were itching to help."

"You can touch me like that anytime." He wished he could call the words back. It was too much. Her face had paled.

He needed to take her mind off what he'd said. "Why don't you go get your dinner? I've got something to check and I'll be just a minute."

"Okay."

After she left, Jake closed his eyes and took a deep breath, willing his body to forget the feel of her hands on his body. It wasn't easy. He craved Sammie's hands, and wanted them reaching lower than his neck and shoulders. His hands tingled with the need to do the same to her.

Not helping. He rolled his head, drew in a couple more breaths, more under control to face Sammie.

Headed to the kitchen, dished up food and sat across

from her

Sam glowed. She'd changed since arriving on the ranch. The scared, pale waif was mostly gone. "Abby and I went for a ride today. Adam came along. I was even more comfortable on a horse this time. I think I used to enjoy riding."

"I want you to always take me or one of the hands. We get the occasional rustler, but if your horse threw you, we'd never know where to look."

"Ok, I'll remember, Jake." Sam played with her food like she wanted to say something. She gave him a quick glance then dropped her eyes to her food. "Abby told me that you took her in after her husband beat her."

"Yeah, I responded to the call. He got a little roughed up when I was trying to get him cuffed and into the back of my car." He shouldn't feel satisfaction from injuring a man he was arresting. "I waited with Abby for the ambulance. She didn't have anywhere to go and she was afraid of her husband, now her ex. Once she got out of the hospital, I offered her the position here. We'd been without a housekeeper for weeks and the guys were getting desperate for a good meal." He smiled.

"And—" Sam smiled "—there was no way that husband of hers was going to come here and hurt her again."

"That's right. She's safe here, just like you are."

"Why do you keep reminding me I'm safe here?"

Jake stilled. He couldn't tell her what had happened to her; she was blocking it for a reason. He didn't want to be the one to make her remember something she obviously didn't want to.

"Having no memory of your life must be kind of scary. I just want you to be comfortable here and not worry about anything." He wasn't sure if she notice how fearful she was around his men. Maybe it felt normal for her.

She touched his hand and pulled back. "Thank you,

51

Jake. I *am* comfortable here."

~~~

She sat on the lumpy bed, her left wrist shackled to the rail behind her. Three strips of old plywood covered the window, letting in light along two three-inch gaps, revealing the scarred wood floor and dust bunnies. The room was otherwise empty.

A door slammed in another part of the house and her breath caught. She didn't know why they'd taken her, but so far she hadn't been hurt. Footsteps pounded up the stairs and the door flung open. She stared at the pretty face with the dimples and leer.

"I won't be needing this anymore." He dropped a ski mask and it landed on the floor beside his foot. Her heart pounded. They'd worn masks when bringing her meals, the only times they came into the room. Something had changed for him to let her see him. They weren't going to let her go.

He stalked toward her. "Daddy won't play, so now it's your turn."

She slammed her back against the rails, painfully cutting into her ribs. She clutched her free fist against her chest. "No! No! Please, no."

"No! No! Please, no. No! No!"

He grabbed her shoulder. "Sammie, wake up! Sammie." A hand ran gently down her cheek. Her heart pounded. The pain would start soon and he would enjoy it. She flinched away from the touch and opened her eyes, trying to catch her breath. The hand left her shoulder, and she should feel relief, but this time, she wanted it back.

"Sammie, it's Jake. Are you all right?"

She grabbed his hand and held it tight to her chest. She closed her eyes. "He-he-he—" She shook her head. She didn't know. Some kind of nightmare had scared her. She was afraid it wasn't a bad dream, but a memory that filled her with terror.

"Did you remember something?" His brows came down, over his sleepy eyes.

She shook her head and squeezed his hand. "No. I can't. I don't want to. I just know it was horrible."

Trembling took over her whole body. Two-thirty. Sleep would never come after that nightmare. She was afraid she'd relive it.

"Jake, can you stay with me until I fall asleep?"

His voice was barely above a whisper. "Sure, sunshine." He sat beside the bed, his eyes level with her.

She curled onto her side, not releasing his hand and rested her other arm across his arm, her lips inches from their twined hands. She dragged in deep breaths in hopes it would ease the trembling. She concentrated on the heat that his arm offered. She was safe with Jake. He could protect her even from bad dreams.

"Sweet dreams, sunshine."

Chapter 10

Jake sorted through the papers on his desk. The one he'd been reading the night before was missing. His brain was muddled from being yanked from sleep and staying beside Sammie for over an hour. It honored him that she trusted him enough to fall asleep after her nightmare. He would have stayed up all night if she needed him.

His mind reviewed his actions of the evening before, then remembered the paper was on his nightstand.

At the top of the stairs, the sound of breaking glass stopped him. He raced down to Sam's bedroom and knocked on the door. "Sammie, you okay?"

She didn't answer. Maybe the memory from the nightmare had come back to her. If he entered, he could scare her, but maybe she'd hurt herself. The wrong move could hurt her emotionally Her cry galvanized him.

He opened the door and stepped in. The cry came from the bathroom. "Sammie?" He stepped up to the door and found her naked, her hands covering her face and surrounded by the glass remnants. He averted his eyes, not wanting her to find him staring at her while she was so vulnerable. He grabbed the towel off the bar and wrapped it around her. "I'm going to carry you into the other room so you don't get cut."

Through sniffles she said, "Jake, I'm sorry I broke the glass."

"You think I'm concerned about a glass?" He set her down beside the bed and wrapped her robe around her.

"Here, put your arms through the sleeves and you can drop the towel." Once he tied it, he sat her on the bed and eased down beside her.

"You're not crying over a broken glass. What happened?" He held her hands and tried to convey his concern.

"After my shower, I was reaching behind me to put anti-itch ointment on a mosquito bite on my back. My skin was lumpy all around it, so I turned to look over my shoulder in the mirror." Fresh tears streamed down her face.

Jake's mouth became a straight line as he waited for her to continue. "And?"

"My back is covered in scars. I spun around because I didn't want to see it anymore and-and I knocked the glass down."

He'd forgotten the doctor had told him about the scars. "I'm so sorry."

Without thought, he pulled her into his arms, then worried about her reaction. She didn't fight him, but left her hands in her lap.

"Would you mind if I looked at your back?" He didn't need to see it, but her reaction made him want to better understand.

She stiffened.

"You can hold the towel in front of you and I'll lower your robe off your shoulders."

She stared at him for several seconds then dropped her gaze to her hands for a moment longer, and picked up the towel. She turned her back to him, loosened her belt, and held the towel against the front of her.

He slowly eased the robe off her shoulders. He had to stifle a gasp. He didn't want her to hear how it affected him. The scars covered her back from just under her arms to her butt. Some were thin lines, others thicker. None of them were recent. He slipped the robe back up in place. "Oh, sunshine." He hugged her again. "You don't remember them do you?"

She shook her head. "What do you think caused them?"

He pulled back and studied her. "Do you really want to know? This might be a reason for your amnesia."

"You're scaring me." Fresh tears rimmed her eyes.

"I'm sorry. I don't mean to. I'll only tell you if you're serious about finding out."

She closed her eyes. Indecision crossed her face. A frown, a firm mouth. She pulled in a deep breath and opened her eyes. Tears still shimmered but her voice was firm. "Tell me."

It was his turn to hesitate. The therapist wouldn't be happy with his untrained help. Maybe it would cause a setback. He stared into her eyes as he spoke. "You've been whipped." Her eyebrows rose. "Repeatedly." She frowned. "Over a long time. And it wasn't recent."

"Why would someone do something like that to another person?"

He relaxed a little. Her response seemed clinical, as if the abuse had happened to someone else. In a way, it had.

"For control. A parent over a child. A husband over a wife. A captor over his victim." Although her more recent trauma didn't include whipping, he threw in the captor part to see if it made any memories click.

"I can't imagine someone wanting to control another person that way." She shivered. "What now?"

"Nothing really changes, unless it helps you remember who you are." He lifted his eyebrows. "Anything?"

She shook her head. "I don't know if I want to remember something like that."

Her despair hurt him.

"I have valid reasons for having amnesia, don't I?" She caught her bottom lip between her teeth.

"Yeah, you do." He touched her face. "Sunshine, you just have to take this one day at a time. You're stronger than when you first got here. You aren't as tense as you were at first." He smiled and touched her cheek.

She covered his hand. "You're a very patient man. Thank you."

His fear of causing her pain made him the most patient man on Earth.

Chapter 11

Jake mused over what Paul had told him at their meeting that morning. The ranch hands had been training a new horse and Sam had been spending a lot of time at the paddock watching them. She'd started talking to the men, asking the reasons for some of the steps in training. A few times one of the men would approached her while he was on Raven's back and she was so interested in the horse, she allowed him near her. His foreman told him the last ride Sam took, she allowed him to ride with them instead of trailing behind, although on the other side of Abby. The three of them had a nice conversation and Sam seemed normal and comfortable.

Jake was happy Sam was coming out of her shell and not as afraid anymore. He hoped that these new memories she was making would help her deal with her old life when or if she remembered it.

He leaned forward in his chair and popped up the missing persons reports. He did it automatically every morning, but was beginning to feel it was worthless. No one reported someone missing four months after they disappeared.

He jumped through the pictures. Sadly, there were always so many new ones every day.

His heart skipped a beat.

Was that?

He flew back two pictures and stared at Sammie's face. The saddest eyes stared at him, no smile on her face. It was like she wasn't there. Nothing like the Sammie he'd come to know with smiles that lit up with her personality.

Finding her picture after all this time made his heart skip a beat. He might lose her. He threw a pencil across the room. No one was getting their hands on her unless they had a good reason for not reporting her missing. And not until he was confident this person wasn't responsible for her mistreatment.

Her name was Samantha Hollingsworth. She *had* remembered it correctly. Her brother, Benjamin filed the report. Heat filled him and cold pushed it out.

Maybe, once Sammie talked to her brother, she'd remember everything about her life. She wouldn't need him anymore. She would go back to her previous life. He looked back at her eyes. He reached out and caressed her cheek. But what kind of life had she had, if this was the picture that was posted? There was no joy.

Maybe knowing about her brother would make her want to go back to her old life. His chest constricted. He didn't want her to leave. Many times throughout his work day, he wondered what Sammie was doing, if she needed him. His first thought before he left work at the end of his shift was what he would do to make her smile. Maybe he was just a crutch for her, a helping hand before she stepped back into that other life.

Jake's hand hovered over the phone. He almost didn't want to call. No one would know he'd found her picture. She could build a new life without all the baggage from her past.

He gripped the handset, his finger hovered over the dial then he pushed the first number, his heart hammering as he finished.

After two rings, it was picked up. "Albany missing persons."

"This is Sheriff Jake Hamilton in Willow Ridge, Arkansas. I believe we've found one of your missing persons."

They spent many minutes discussing all Jake knew of Sam's disappearance. With a promise to send all the evidence they'd collected, he finally got the phone number for Sammie's brother.

It was easier to dial this time, but only because he'd already started it rolling.

"Hello."

"Is this Benjamin Hollingsworth?"

"Yes, who am I talking to?"

"This is Sheriff Jake Hamilton. I have some questions on the report you filed yesterday."

There was a gasp. "Have you found Sammie?" He called her Sammie. So this was the person that Sam felt love for. Jake was somewhat relieved.

"I need answers first. Why did it take you four months to report her missing?"

"Yeah, that does look bad doesn't it? I've been out of the country for four months. I just got back two days ago. Sammie and I had an argument just before I left. One of her coworkers had been beaten and I was trying again to talk her into taking a job near me, outside of that ghetto she works in. So, I figured she was just mad at me and wouldn't answer my calls. It did get ridiculously longer than usual, but I didn't know how else to reach her."

Jake clenched his hand. It seemed the only person who cared had been unavailable.

"When I got back, I went to her apartment. It looked like she hadn't been there in a long time. Dead plants, spoiled milk. I asked a couple of neighbors who said they hadn't seen her in months. Then I went to her work. It's a social services agency. They told me she'd quit. So she *had* listened to me and got out. They also gave me the address for her new employer, a private child psychologist's office. I went there and they said that she'd only shown up for a few days and they never saw her again. They never pursued it when she didn't show up."

Ben's voice rasped. "The sad thing is the social services people would have reported her missing if she'd still been working there and disappeared. She changed jobs at the wrong time." His anguish showed in his voice.

Jake closed his eyes and pulled in a breath. "You're right. Something did happen. From what we've pieced together, she was kidnapped."

"Pieced together?" Ben wailed. "She's dead?"

"No! Sorry. I should have said that differently. She has amnesia. We're guessing she was held for about three months."

Ben's sharply indrawn breath hissed in Jake's ear. "Oh, my God. Poor Sammie. I guess dear old Dad didn't come through with the ransom. How were the kidnappers to know that he wouldn't pay?"

"Who *is* your father?"

Ben sneered. "Jeffery P. Hollingsworth the second. Great financier on Wall Street."

"So, you think that your father wouldn't pay rather than the exchange fell apart?"

Ben's voice hardened. "That's exactly what I think. When we were growing up, we had bodyguards. I overheard Dad more than once telling them to protect us well because ransom was not an option. If I'd known, I would have done anything to get her back." He was agitated.

"How—" Ben cleared his throat. "How did she escape?"

"I found her in an overturned van. She'd been badly beaten, brutally raped and barely escaped with her life. That's all we know. Does she have other family?" Like a husband.

"No, just me. *He* doesn't count. I wouldn't blame her if

she never gets her memory back. How is she now?"

"She's physically better. She's getting happier and less wary of men."

"She's always been wary of men. She never dates. I never understood it." Ben took a deep breath. "I'm glad she's happy. She hasn't really been happy since I left home. I guess you could say she's never ruffled. Nothing excites her; nothing makes her angry. Except for with the children she sees in her practice. She cares very much for them and works hard to help them heal from their emotional trauma. But even then, she never gets truly excited when she talks about their accomplishments."

That sounded nothing like his Sammie. It was as if her lack of bad memories allowed the real woman to shine through. "Ben, do you know how she got the scars on her back? It looks like she's been whipped." Several seconds of silence followed.

"No! I can't believe he did that to her. She never told me. If she had, I would have found a way to get her out of there."

"Who?"

"Our father. I'm sure my back looks as bad as hers. He always verbally abused us. He used to whip me. He had a special belt in his bedroom closet just for that. But he never touched Sammie. I left home as soon as I finished high school. Sammie was thirteen. I would never have left if I'd thought he was going to start whipping her," he said, vehemently.

"What about your mother? Did she try to stop it?"

"Mom died when I was eight. Dad started whipping me shortly after that."

"Why didn't you go to the authorities?" Jake tapped a pencil eraser on his desk.

"I tried once when I was ten. I went to the counselor at

our prestigious private school. She didn't believe me. Why would a man as rich as Dad do something like that? He was more careful with whipping at that point so I didn't have scars yet."

Jake pulled in a deep breath, tamping down hatred for a man he'd never met. A child should be able to trust a parent to keep her safe.

"I'd like to see her," said Ben.

"I think you should talk to Sammie's psychologist first." He worried that Sammie's recognition of her brother would make too many memories rush back at once. He couldn't imagine how overwhelming that might be.

"Yeah, that makes sense. I feel so helpless."

"I'd like to give your number to her psychologist so she can talk to you. You may be able to help her understand Sammie better."

"Of course. I'd do anything for my baby sister."

After hanging up the phone, Jake sat back in his chair. He agreed with Ben. Sammie would be better off without getting her memory back. She'd had too much pain in her life.

He'd realized in passing that Sammie didn't have a husband or boyfriend, intensifying the feelings that had been building up over the last month. She didn't have anyone to go back to.

He picked up the phone again, and called Dr. Reynolds, telling her what he'd learned.

"Finally Sam has a name."

"Yeah, but not one she wants. Doctor, I have a feeling she'd be better off never getting her memory back. Her brother said she was never happy, maybe even emotionless. Sam's been happy, even excited recently. I'd hate to see that change if she starts remembering. She deserves better."

"You're right. She's happy. I think without all the

baggage, she's had a chance to be the woman she was always meant to be. She's gotten stronger and hopefully she's strong enough to deal with her past, if she does remember it."

Jake sighed. "I guess we'll have to wait and see."

His next call was to Jeffery P. Hollingsworth the second. "Good Morning, Hollingsworth Holdings."

"I'd like to speak with Jeffery Hollingsworth. This is Sheriff Jake Hamilton."

"Just a moment, sir."

Waiting to talk to this man who could inflict such pain on his children caused his anger to rise. He should have left it to Alex to call. He'd been too impatient to find out more about Sammie.

Several seconds later she came back on. "Sheriff, what is this regarding?"

"His daughter, Samantha."

"Just a moment."

"This is Jeffery Hollingsworth. What can I do for you, Sheriff?"

"Mr. Hollingsworth, I'm calling in regards to your daughter, Samantha."

"Have you found her?"

"Yes, she's alive, but she has amnesia."

"She's alive?"

"With no help from you. Was she kidnapped a few months ago? Did someone demand ransom?"

After several seconds of silence, Jake raised his voice. "Did you receive a ransom demand?"

"Yes! I refuse to pay ransoms."

"So, you resigned your daughter to torture and death without even trying to save her?"

"I was in a difficult position and the chance of a safe recovery of a kidnap victim isn't that great."

"You could have at least tried, Mr. Hollingsworth. Why

didn't you report her kidnapping to the police?"

"They wouldn't have been able to do anything, except crawl all over my home and office and insist I give in to the demands."

Jake couldn't take any more of the man's selfishness. He hung up.

Sammie's own father had turned his back on her, putting a higher value on his money than her life. Jake had only known her a short time and would do anything to keep her from harm.

Jake sat back in his chair, concentrating on his breathing until he calmed enough to function. He had one more call to make. "Alex, this is Jake."

"Hi, Jake. What's up?"

"I found a missing person report on Sam today. Her name is Samantha Hollingsworth, daughter of Jeffery P. Hollingsworth, rich guy on Wall Street."

Alex whistled.

"Her brother just got back into the country and reported her missing." He relayed the details he'd learned from Ben. "Sorry, I also called the father. I should have left it to you. Anyway, Sam *was* kidnapped and he refused to pay ransom."

"He didn't even report it? What a bastard."

"Yeah. He's also the one who put those scars on her back and her brother's, too."

Alex swore again. "Okay, thanks. I'll give the father a call and see if we can trace the kidnapper's call. It was probably too short or a burner phone, but I might as well try. And find out exactly what they said to him."

"Thanks, Alex." Jake gave him both the father and brother's phone numbers.

Jake strode from his office. "Dannie, I'm going home."

"But, Sheriff—"

He held up his hand. "I just can't deal with anything

more today." He relented. "You can call me if anything comes up that you can't handle."

He stalked out the door. He hoped the ride home would calm him enough to not upset Sammie with his anger.

Chapter 12

Jake pulled into his regular parking spot. Sam stood at the paddock, watching Steve train Raven. She turned when he was almost beside her and her eyes widened.

"Jake, you're home." Her eyes lit up and she wrapped an arm around his waist and turned back to watch the training. He put his arm around her shoulder and she tipped her head against him.

Just a few weeks ago, if he'd walked up to her like that, fear would have filled her eyes until she saw who it was. She'd come so far. He kissed the top of her head, and she smiled up at him.

"Do you want to go for a ride?" he asked.

Her eyes lit up. "Always. Race you to the barn."

He laughed as he followed her at a slower pace.

"I want to change into jeans first."

"Okay. I'll start saddling the horses."

When Jake returned, he was carrying a blanket, two canteens, and a sack lunch. He stowed them away.

"Jake, can you check that I've done everything right?"

"Sure thing, sunshine." The only thing he needed to do was synch the saddle tighter on his horse. "You did great. Are you ready to go?"

"Yeah." Sam mounted her horse. "Can we go to the river?"

"Of course." He mounted and led the way.

They talked for a while before Sam said, "Abby told me her sister is coming to visit. She came last summer for a couple of weeks."

"I think she's got one more year of college left. Are you okay with her being here?"

"Yes. It's easier thinking about her sister coming rather than if it had been a brother." Her voice softened. "It made me wonder if I have any siblings. And if I do, why aren't they trying to find me?"

Jake's chest constricted around his heart. Sam had a hole in her life that he could help fill. "I discovered something today."

Damn! He spoke before he thought it through. He should leave it to Dr. Reynolds to tell her.

Sam lifted her eyebrows expectantly. She frowned. "Jake, what did you discover?"

He turned his face to the sky so he didn't have to look at her. "I spoke too soon. I don't know if I should say."

She stopped her horse and dismounted. One hand held the reins and the other dropped to her hip. "Jake, you can't start to give me something and then yank it away." Her stern face stared back at him.

He was torn. He jumped off his horse and stepped toward her.

She crossed her arms, reins tangling. An avenging angel on a mission. "You have to tell me."

"All right. But not until we get to the river, and eat. I need time to think about the best way to tell you." And how much.

Standing on her toes, she gave him a kiss beside his mouth then climbed onto her horse. She stared straight ahead.

Jake was in shock. Sammie just kissed him. It wasn't a sexy kiss, but still, it was a kiss. He mounted his horse and they moved into a trot. What was the purpose of the kiss? Maybe it promised something more. He hoped she didn't regret doing it.

He flicked a glance to her. She stared straight ahead, maybe regretting her action. For now, he'd pretend it didn't happen.

~~~

Sam couldn't believe what she'd done. She'd kissed Jake! It wasn't on the mouth. It could be taken for a brotherly kiss, but still she'd kissed him. She cared for him. She was more comfortable with him than anybody, but she probably shouldn't have done it. She couldn't look at him. She didn't want to see a puzzled expression, or one expecting something more than she was able to give, or a closed off face that wished she hadn't done it.

She was falling in love with him, but had nothing to compare it to. Maybe it was gratitude. There was certainly that. Not many people would take in a stranger for who knew how long. He was patient with her. He knew exactly what to say or do to make her feel better. So, she was definitely grateful, but did it go beyond that? Love? Maybe if she'd had a memory of loving someone she'd know. But all she had were new memories of only a few weeks.

The rest of the ride, Jake was quiet. Sam had to get his attention each time she wanted to ask him something. She finally gave up.

They arrived at the river, and Jake spread the blanket, set the sack of food on it, then sat. Sam stood beside her horse. She was no longer a pale ghost. She didn't think she'd ever had skin as golden as now.

He raised his brows. "Come eat."

"But what about—"

"We'll eat first and then I'll tell you."

She sighed and pointed a finger at him. "You better!"

She sat beside him as he pulled food out. He talked about everything but what Sam wanted to know.

"Okay, I'm done." Sam stuffed a piece of crust back into the plastic bag.

Jake smiled and took two more bites to finish his sandwich. He put all their leftovers back into the saddle bag and returned to her.

"Sammie, I found your picture on the missing person reports this morning."

She gasped and put her fingers over her mouth, tears welling. Someone cared enough to try to find her. It shouldn't have taken so long, but still, someone was out there who cared. "Someone's looking for me? You—you know who I am?" She closed her eyes. Her old life had seemed so far away, and now it loomed over her. Maybe she had an ogre for a husband.

"I already know who you are. I know what makes you smile, what makes you laugh, what makes you sad. I know what you like to do for fun, what you find a challenge. I think I already know the important things."

She smiled, and touched his cheek. "Thank you, Jake. That means a lot to me." She pulled in a deep breath and whooshed it out. "Do I have a full name? Am I really Sam?"

Jake narrowed his eyes, as if studying her. "Your full name is Samantha Hollingsworth." He waited for it to sink in.

Sam frowned. She tumbled the name in her head and shivered. "I don't like Samantha. It's a pretty name, but when I say it in my head, it makes me cringe."

Jake took her hand. "I also talked to your brother. He's the one who reported you missing."

She squeezed his hand. "A brother? But why did he take so long to report me missing?"

"He called you Sammie. He's been out of the country for

months and the first thing he did when he got back was try to find you and then reported you missing."

She smiled. "What's his name? Did you like him?"

Jake returned her smile. "Yeah, I liked him. He really cares about you. His name is Ben."

"Ben. Ben." She rolled his name around a few times. "My mouth can feel that I've said that name." A thought popped into her head. "Sometimes I call him Jay." She gave him the biggest smile he'd yet seen. "Ben-Jay-man. Can you tell me anything else about him?"

"I've probably told you more than I should have. Why don't we leave it at that for now and see if anything else comes to you?"

"You're probably right." Sam smiled. "I have a brother." Family.

Sam leaned back on her arms and tipped her head to the sun. "I love it out here. The gurgle of the river is calming. Sometimes I can hear the cattle in the distance. I feel so safe here." Just the word that Jake kept using. It did fit and she didn't know why. Maybe her brother would help her figure it out.

~~~

Jake studied Sammie while her eyes were closed. She was beautiful. She'd changed so much since she'd arrived—more carefree, no fearful hesitate as if afraid she'd do wrong.

She had gotten under his skin. More than that, she had wiggled her way into his heart. He wanted to touch her, but he needed to give her time. She'd been through more than she knew and he didn't want to cause her fears to return.

There was always the chance that remembering her previous life would send her into a tailspin. Or maybe Sammie would want to return to that life, leaving him

71

behind.

No matter what happened, he wouldn't regret taking her in and providing a safe place for her to recover. Even if he might not.

Chapter 13

The following morning Jake placed another call to Dr. Reynolds. He explained to her how he'd told Sam about her brother and her reaction.

"I hadn't really intended to tell her, but she was wondering about her family because my housekeeper's sister is coming. It just slipped out."

"I don't think it's harmed her. I talked to Ben yesterday and I have a fuller understanding of Sam's life. I plan on talking to her about her brother and maybe in a couple of weeks, we can have him come visit her."

"Take it slow, Doctor. I know she's not as fragile as she was, but I'm worried about how she'd react if she remembers how her father treated her."

"It's certainly a risk. When I talked to Ben, I got the sense that he loves her and she needs that in her life to help her rebuild memories. She's nearly a clean slate. She's got vague emotions she doesn't understand, but she doesn't have the memories that go with them. It helps her to accept those emotions and deal with them. She'll be stronger than she was before."

~~~

A few weeks later, Jake watched Sammie push her breakfast around on her plate and she'd barely said a word. He'd gotten used to her exuberance in the morning, as she talked about her plans.

"You okay, sunshine?"

She caught her bottom lip between her teeth. "I'm nervous and I'm excited. I don't know how I'll last until one o'clock when Stacey brings Ben to my session. And I'm afraid of how I'll react when I see him. We've talked about him. He even sent a picture of himself. But I only remember bits and pieces about him." Her eyes misted with tears. "What if I see him and my whole life rushes back in? I don't know if I could take that."

Jake touched her temple. "Your brain is only going to give you what you're ready to deal with." He sure hoped that was true. He didn't want her to have a breakdown. "Do you want me to stay home today?"

Her smile trembled, and she grasped his hand. "No. But thank you for the offer. I trust Stacey. But would you mind coming home early? I don't know how I'll be afterward and-and –"

When confusion crossed her face, Jake squeezed her hand. "How about if I get here about three-thirty?"

Jake's heart did a little flip at the look of relief on her face.

~~~

Pins and needles? Who was she kidding? Spikes and nails dogged Sam through the morning. She ate lunch with Abby in the kitchen. All ranch hands were in a far pasture, so they were alone. Her excitement twisted her stomach and she couldn't eat much.

The doorbell rang, and Sam's heart rate spiked. Even though it was time for her appointment with Stacey, Sam always had to peek through the window beside the door to make sure. Stacey stood there with the man from the photo behind her. She pulled in a breath and opened the door. She stared at the stranger, being anything but the polite hostess.

A grin spread across his face and she might have detected tears in his eyes. "Sammie."

That voice belonged in warm dreams, filling her heart with love—for him and from him. She flattened her hand over her heart. She stepped onto the porch and wrapped him in a hug. It took them both by surprise. She'd hugged Jake a couple of times, but it made her nervous. With this man, somewhere inside, she remembered that he loved her.

"Come to the living room." Stacey sat in a chair and Ben took one side of the couch. She remembered she should be a hostess, even though she'd never offered Stacey anything before. "Would either of you like something to drink?"

They both declined, so Sam sat on the opposite end of the couch from Ben.

Stacey's gaze darted between them. "Sam, I'm surprised you hugged Ben. Do you remember more about him?"

She gave a side-glance to him, but kept her focus on Stacey. "Just those bits I told you about. But when I saw him, I felt his love for me. And mine for him. I didn't think I had family when Jake couldn't find a report about me, so it felt wonderful to find Ben."

Stacey directed her gaze to Ben. "What about you, Ben? How did you feel when Sam hugged you?"

His eyebrows popped up. It sounded to her like he was getting the psychologist grilling, and she didn't understand why.

"I, uh. Sammy hasn't hugged me in years. It took me by surprise. And her face glowed with happiness." He faced Sam and didn't speak until she looked at him. "And it felt good to have my sister hug me."

She frowned. "I didn't hug you? Shouldn't brothers and sisters hug?"

He shrugged. "We didn't after I left home."

"How old were we when you left?"

"I was eighteen. You were thirteen. You changed after that. I should have questioned it."

Her heart pounded, and cold enveloped her body. This was headed somewhere she didn't want it to go. Forbidden territory that needed to stay hidden. "Stacey—"

"Let's move this to your early childhood." Stacey's smooth, steady voice calmed Sam.

"Ben, why don't you start a story that maybe Sam can remember."

He squinted and then his eyes cleared. "It was your sixth birthday. I asked Mrs. Brownwell to make you a birthday cake. She made a small chocolate one big enough for two. We had a tea party in your playroom and had the cake. I wasn't allowed to buy you a present, so I gave you my stuffed red fox."

"Red Tail. I remember him." She didn't remember the party, but she felt the comfort she got from the stuffed animal. Her brother must have been the best ever.

"You slept with him for years."

He told her about friends she had, but none of them jogged a memory.

Ben grinned. "How about this one? I got a car for my sixteenth birthday, but I wasn't allowed to take you out for a ride. You kept begging me to give you a ride, so we rode up and down the driveway and once around the house. I got my car taken away for two weeks for that, but it was worth it."

She scrunched her eyes. "I don't remember." She wished she did. It sounded like Ben was the best part of her life. At least until she'd met Jake.

Ben told her a few more stories, but it was as if he talked about a stranger.

He took her hand. "Tell me what's been happening with

you."

"Jake asked me to come stay on the ranch. He's so nice. Everybody here is. I've been riding. I can't remember doing it, but I knew how."

He grinned. "You've always loved it. Dad boarded horses for us at a nearby stable and we went there as often as we were allowed."

Sam wished she could remember riding with Ben. In the short time they'd talked, she knew she loved him.

Stacey had let the two of them chat without interrupting. "I think it's time we headed out. Sam, after meeting Ben, you may find some more memories surface. If you have any problems with them, give me a call."

They stood and Ben hugged her. "Come stay with me. Let me help you."

The request didn't strike fear in her, but she felt uncomfortable at the thought of leaving. Part of it was that she'd leave Jake behind, but also that she would no longer feel safe.

She tightened the hug and stepped back. "Thank you for inviting me, but I'm not ready for that. This is where I need to be right now."

"All right. But I'd like to talk to you on the phone."

They exchanged numbers and said their goodbyes. A piece of Sam's old life was falling into place. The only part she wanted to remember.

~~~

Jake returned home that afternoon and found Sammie sitting on the porch swing. He opened his truck door and she flew down the steps, throwing herself at him. He was glad he'd seen a smile on her face before she buried it in his chest. His arms enclosed her, wishing she could stay there forever.

"How did it go, sunshine?"

Sam lifted her head and smiled. "It went really well. I like my brother." She stepped out of his arms and took his hand. She led him to the porch swing and they sat. She backed herself into the corner with her knees pulled up under her chin. Jake dropped his arm onto the back of the seat.

He ran a finger up and down Sam's arm. "Well, of course he was interested in what his sister's been doing. So, you're glad you did this?"

"Yes! We've even arranged for him to come back in a couple of weeks." Sam dropped her eyes to her feet and then back up at Jake. "You don't mind that I stay longer, do you?"

It tore at him that someday, maybe soon, she'd be ready to leave. He was helping her heal and it was her decision if or when she left. He couldn't make the choice for her, but he hoped she would stay.

He put his hand on her arm. "Stay as long as you want."

She gave him a wobbly smile. "W-would you mind if Ben stays here for a day or two?"

"That would be great, as long as Dr. Reynolds thinks it's okay."

She took the hand he'd placed on her arm and kissed his fingers. "Thank you, Jake." She kissed them again and his breath quickened.

This was not a good idea.

He should pull his hand away. Her eyes told him she wanted more, but he knew she wasn't ready. As much as he wanted to kiss her, he had to be strong.

She scooted closer and draped her legs across his lap. Her fingers skimmed his cheek, then her lips touched his.

This was so not a good idea.

His arm had a brain of its own as it came around her back and pulled her closer. Sam slid her hand through his hair and kissed him again. Jake groaned and returned her kiss.

This was *so* not a good idea.

He teased her lips with his tongue and was surprised when she opened to him. He deepened the kiss.

She was affected as much as he was. It took everything in him to not carry her up to his bed. He slowly backed off, giving her quick feathery kisses. He tipped his head up and tucked hers against his neck. His arms didn't want to release her, but she wasn't ready for intimacy. Just like her memories, they'd have to take it slow.

Jake kissed the top of Sam's head, and let out a long breath. "Sammie, you feel so good in my arms." She slanted her head just enough to give him a kiss at the base of his neck.

He held her for a few more minutes, and did the hard thing, suggesting they go eat dinner.

Chapter 14

Jake's office phone rang. "Sheriff Hamilton." He propped the phone against his neck while he flipped through a folder.

"Sheriff, this is Ben Hollingsworth." Jake straightened and grabbed the phone.

"Ben, call me Jake. Sammie told me about the wonderful visit she had with you yesterday. What can I do for you?"

"Jake, I just called to thank you for how much you're helping Sammie. She's a different person. She's happy. She was so excited when she was telling me about the ranch."

"She's come a long way. I don't know that I'm doing anything special. I'm just making sure she stays safe."

"But it's more than that. I think that without memories of her horrible childhood, she's becoming the person she was meant to be. You've helped her to do that. She wouldn't be where she is if she was living at that women's shelter Stacey told me about."

"With Sammie's fragile state of mind, I couldn't let her go there." The connection he had with her wouldn't allow it.

"Not many would take in a stranger, so thank you. After I moved away from home, Sammie started avoiding touch. At the time, I thought she withdrew since we didn't see each other very often after that. But it was probably because of what our father did to her. You can imagine how surprised I was when she hugged me yesterday. The last time she did that was the day I moved out."

"I'm glad I'm making a difference. Sammie mentioned

that you're coming back for a couple of days. You're welcome to stay on the ranch. It'll give you more time to spend with her."

"Thank you. I appreciate it."

Jake set the phone in its cradle and leaned back. He'd suspected the kidnapping had traumatized her, not that she'd avoided touch before that. It had taken a few weeks for her to become comfortable with him and the others, and he thought she was recovering from her recent trauma. Instead, starting fresh with new memories gave her a second chance to blossom. She worked with Abby and they talked and laughed together. She'd grown comfortable with the ranch hands, and even joked with them. What he liked best was that she seemed to enjoy touching him. He did, too, probably more than he should. Sammie, and now her brother, trusted him to keep her safe. And that included from himself.

~~~

"You're all bubbly today," Jake smiled as Sam wiggled in her chair at the dining room table like a child.

She intertwined her fingers. "I can hardly wait until Ben gets here. Talking on the phone with him has been so nice, but it's not the same." Sam stared down at her fingers then at Jake. "I told Abby that we'd have lunch with the guys today."

He frowned at her nervousness. "I don't mind if you eat in here with Ben."

Sam squeezed his hand. "This will be the first time I'm eating with the hands."

He'd kept tabs on her, asking Abby about her progress. She'd always eaten lunch in his office or before the men came in.

"I thought it was time to join the guys. There are fewer of them here at lunchtime and Ben will be with me, too. It'll give him a chance to meet them."

"If that's what you want. It's a good next step." Maybe this was how Jake would lose her—one small step at a time.

"Exactly. I felt like I was just getting stuck and I needed to push myself a little."

"You can take Ben for a ride this afternoon." Her excitement brought a smile to his lips.

She clasped her hands. "That's a great idea. I can show him my favorite places."

"He's not familiar with the dangers, so I want you to still take a ranch hand with you."

~~~

The last day of Ben's visit, Jake arrived home as Sam and Ben sat on the porch swing. Sam laughed at something her brother said.

Jake strode up the steps and sat on the porch rail near them. "Did you two have a good day?"

"Yeah," said Sam. "I'm enjoying getting to know Ben again."

"I can smell dinner. You ready to eat?" Jake gazed between Ben and Sam.

Sam's stomach growled and she laughed. "Ben, do you mind eating dinner with the guys?"

"I'm good with it," he said as he stood.

Jake was surprised. The last two nights Ben and Sam had joined him in his office for dinner. Sammie's comfortable level around the men had leaped during Ben's visit. He followed them into the house.

All the hands were present except Andy, who had a date. The guys didn't make a big deal of Sam joining them.

Conversations covered many topics, from what was happening at the ranch and in town to high school sports. Jake had missed these meals with his ranch hands although he wouldn't have traded all the private meals that he and Sammie had shared.

The meal ended and Ben held Sam's hand. "I've got to catch my plane. I hope it won't be too long before we see each other again."

She hugged him. "I'm so glad you could visit."

"You could come visit me."

Sam's shoulders hunched as she pushed away from Ben. She shook her head. "I-I'm not ready yet."

Ben touched her cheek. "It's okay. I'm not pushing."

She nodded and sucked in a breath.

The three of them headed out. Ben picked up the bag he'd left beside the front door and they accompanied him to his car. Sam gave him another quick hug and stepped back.

Ben took her hand. "I've enjoyed spending time with you and discovering the new Sammie. I'm glad you're doing so well."

"I'm glad you're my family, Ben."

Jake held out his hand and Ben shook it. "Thanks for coming to visit Sammie."

"Thanks for having me, Jake. It's been a really long time since Sammie and I have spent this much time together. It was nice, even with the holes in her memory." He grinned.

She stuck her tongue out and laughed at his surprised expression.

Jake wrapped an arm around her as Ben drove away. They returned to the house, and she pulled him to the porch swing. She sat in the corner, and pulled her knees up. She wrapped one arm around her legs and took Jake's hand with the other as he sat next to her.

He squeezed it. "What happened when Ben asked you to

visit?" He studied her, hoping he wasn't pushing too much.

"I don't know. I got scared about leaving here. It's like there's something really scary out there and I don't know what it is."

"It's all right. You do what you're comfortable doing."

She sighed and stared at their joined hands. "I persuaded Ben to tell me what happened to my back."

Jake rubbed his thumb across Sam's hand.

"He said our"—she choked on the next word—"father did it." Tears ran down her cheeks. "He said I never told him about it. Why wouldn't I have told him?" The anguish in her eyes ate at him.

He bracketed her face between his hands a wiped the tears on her cheeks with his thumbs. "He told me that he'd been whipped from the time he was eight."

More tears rolled down her cheeks.

"Maybe you were protecting him. Maybe you suspected that he'd be whipped again if he tried to protect you."

"What kind of man does that to his own children?"

"A very bad man, Sammie. I hope you never see him again." If Jake ever met him, he couldn't guarantee that he wouldn't hit the man. He pulled Sammie close and kissed the top of her head.

Sam wiped her eyes and cheeks and her chest expanded against him. "On a brighter note, Ben told me I'm a psychologist. I've been working with children who've been abused. I wonder if I'll get enough memories back to be able to do it again."

"Why don't you ask Dr. Reynolds for some books you can read about psychology? Maybe more specifically, the psychology of abuse. It might bring back your professional memories."

"Jake, that's a great idea!" She threw her arms around his neck.

He pulled her onto his lap and kissed the side of her face. She turned her head and their lips touched. He should just tip his head back away from her. He shouldn't have pulled her onto his lap. Anywhere close to Sammie broke down his control.

Jake groaned and took her mouth with his. She opened to him and he touched his tongue to hers. He cupped her breast with one hand and slid the other up and down her back. Sam moaned, driving him further over the edge. His fingers slipped under her shirt to explore her skin, and he froze when his hand ran over the bumps of her scars.

Sam pulled back from him. "Jake?"

He shook as he pulled in breath and closed his eyes. Sanity was returning. "Sammie, we shouldn't be doing this." He pulled his hand from her shirt.

"You don't want to touch me because my back is all ugly." The hurt in her voice tore a piece from his heart. Tears shimmered in her eyes.

"That's not it, Sammie. It just reminded me of what you've been through and that you're not ready."

"Jake, I'm ready. My only concern before was if I was married and now I know I'm not." Her gaze dropped and then she brought it up to his. "I want you to make love to me."

He studied her. She didn't realize she wasn't ready, but if he didn't make love to her, it might cause some other psychological damage. There was no way to convince her the scars hadn't stopped him. Only one thing would prove to Sammie that her scars didn't affect how he felt about her. She must have guessed his decision because her eyes softened. He was lost, and hoped this wasn't the most colossal mistake of his life. He swooped down and kissed her. She sighed.

Jake abruptly stood with Sam in his arms and she yelped

then giggled. He gave her a quick kiss and strode to the door. She opened it then he strode through and pushed it closed. He took the stairs two at a time and stepped into his room, then kicked his door closed. He eased her down beside his bed.

He tunneled his fingers into her hair and tried to read her expression. "Sammie, tell me again you want this. I can stop now but it will be harder later." At any point, he would stop if she got scared or panicked.

Sam ran her fingers down his cheek. "Jake, I want you." She stood on her toes and touched her lips to his.

He claimed her. His fingers worked the buttons on her shirt and pants, then the zipper rasped down. Her eyes showed no fear, only her need for him. Sam threw her shoulders back to allow the shirt to slide down her arms. Jake unhooked her bra and slipped it off her. He ran his hands up her back and wished he could make it smooth for her. He tore off his clothes and drew her into his arms. He feathered kisses from her mouth to her jaw and along her neck. She shivered and he pulled her closer. They fit together perfectly. He could be satisfied holding her in his arms all night, but she needed more and he'd make sure that this first time would be everything it should be. He pushed her pants lower then gently laid her on his bed and slid her pants the rest of the way off.

"You're beautiful," he told her. Before climbing in beside her, Jake pulled open a drawer and took out a foil pack and placed it on the bed. Then he worshiped her. His lips touched hers then moved to her cheek and beneath her ear. He slid his hands over her breasts and she shivered. She ran her hands over his back. When she moaned his name, he trailed kisses down to her breast while his fingers found her core.

The only time he'd been this nervous during sex was his

first time. It was more crucial than ever before to get this right.

Sammie whispered his name and Jake reclaimed her mouth as his fingers brought her to climax. Jake ripped open the condom and hoped that Sammie really was ready for what was coming next.

He kissed her and learned her body's responses as he built up her excitement again and then covered her body with his. He paused when she stiffened. "You feel so good, Sammie. Open your eyes. Say my name." He needed her right there with him and not lost in nightmares.

She opened her eyes. "Jake." She relaxed and wrapped a leg around his. He continued to caress her as he slowly buried himself in her. Only when Sammie shifted against him did he start to move. It was almost too good to be true, fitting so perfectly together, his heart tripping and soaring. Too quickly, his control gave way and they shattered together.

He rolled to his side and took Sammie with him. He kissed her forehead and she snuggled into him. This was where she should be. His body relaxed and drifted toward sleep.

Whispered words caused his heart to skip a beat. "I love you, Jake."

Maybe it was a dream.

Chapter 15

Jake woke slowly on his side with a comfortable weight leaning into him. He opened his eyes. Oh, yeah. Sammie's head snuggled under his chin. Her butt was... don't even think about it or he might frighten her. He slid a couple of inches away.

His thoughts the night before hadn't gotten as far as how Sammie would react in the morning.

"Mmmm." The loss of his warmth must have disturbed her. She rolled until her shoulder hit his chest. Sam froze. Her eyes flew open. Several quick, shallow breaths rasped through her mouth. She slowly turned her head toward him... and relaxed. She touched his face and smiled. "Morning, Jake."

He caught her hand before she pulled away, brought it to his lips and kissed her fingers. "Are you okay?"

She nodded.

He slid back a little further and turned Sam on her side, facing him. Each breath caused her breasts to press against his chest. Sam blushed when he couldn't stop his body reacting to her. He lifted her chin, kissed her then pulled back. "Do you regret what we did?"

She shook her head. "No. I... You... It was wonderful. I never imagined making love could feel like that."

He chuckled. "It can get better."

Sam's eyes widened. "Really? I don't know if I'm ready for better."

He chuckled. "Do you want to give it a try or do you

want to get up?"

Sam's arm snaked around Jake's neck. "Let's give it a try."

A satisfying while later, and after they'd eaten breakfast, Jake leaned back in his chair. "I thought you might want to explore a cave today."

Sam's mouth dropped open. "Really? Where is it?"

"It's on my land."

"You have a cave? And you haven't taken me to it yet?"

He laughed. Her excitement was infectious. "It takes a while to get there. Why don't you put together lunch and water and I'll collect a blanket and flashlights? We'll meet at the barn."

Jake tightened the last buckle as Sam came out. He stowed the food and water and they climbed on the horses. He headed in a new direction. "My Dad took me to the cave for the first time when I was about eight. His father showed it to him."

"Is it very big?"

"It's not really large, especially when you compare it to the commercial ones. There's a story my Grandpa used to tell me about how he got stuck in it one winter. The day started out sunny. They didn't have weather radar to warn them of coming storms back then. The snow hit so suddenly and so hard, he got disoriented and ended up going the wrong way. He recognized the area near the cave and knew he couldn't make it back to the house. A fallen tree was near the entrance, so he broke off as many branches as he could carry and brought them into the cave. He led his horse inside and made a fire to keep warm. By late morning of the next day, the snow had nearly stopped, so it was time to leave. It took twice as long to get back home because the snow was so deep. Grandpa said that you never saw two happier people than Grandma and Dad when he walked in the door."

"That's wonderful." Her eyes crinkled with her smile. Then it faded. "Jake, I don't have memories like that. I can call up bits and pieces, but not whole stories. Ben's told me stories. But that's all they are. It's like what you just told me, someone else's life. My life started four months ago when you found me. Ben told me our Mom died when I was three. Did I have memories of her? Did she love us? Did I have stories about my grandparents? I don't know. And sometimes I don't want to know. What does that say about me?" Tears glistened in her eyes.

Jake stopped their horses, dismounted and pulled her from her horse. He wrapped her in his arms and she snaked hers around his waist. "Sammie, pretty soon your mind is going to be full of new memories. Maybe you'll remember more old ones, maybe not. What's important is what you do with what you've got now."

Her forehead creased. "I'll try, Jake." She gave him a sexy smile. "And I've got some pretty nice ones from last night and this morning." She dropped her forehead to his chest.

He chuckled and couldn't resist giving her a kiss or two or three. "If we don't stop, we'll never make it to the cave."

~~~

They climbed back on their horses. Jake seemed lost in thought. The landscape changed as they rode. It was somewhat hilly here. Cattle were scattered across a field beyond the windbreak. An outcropping of rocks at the top of a hill caught her attention, and she wondered if they were natural. The longer grass suggested the cattle hadn't grazed here in a while.

It had been a while since either of them spoke, so it startled Sam when Jake did. "We're here."

She studied their surroundings. "Where? I don't see it."

Jake smiled. "It's actually behind that pine tree." He pointed to a tall, lone tree in front of them. Other trees stood a farther away, but it was the only pine and the tallest tree.

"Well, what's that doing here? It looks out of place." There hadn't been any other trees of its kind on all the rides she'd taken.

"Grandpa planted it to hide the entrance, to block the wind and to make it easier for us to find it from farther away."

"Oh." She dismounted.

Jake pulled out the flashlights. He handed one to Sam and took her hand. He led her to the backside of the pine tree. He ducked to get through the entrance.

"Hey look, I don't even have to duck." She laughed—one of the few instances where her height did her a favor.

The floor sloped down and the ceiling rose, so Jake stood after taking a few steps. Sam shone her light in all directions as she inspected the cave.

"Damn, someone's been in here. Someone who's not supposed to be."

Sam turned back to him. "How can you tell?"

"There's been a fire in here."

Sam stared down at the camp ring. "It looks like there've been a lot of fires." She frowned.

Jake flashed his light to the side of the cave where three pieces of wood sat beside the wall. "Yeah, but ever since my Grandpa was in that snowstorm, we've always made sure to keep a good supply of wood. If we're coming out to stay, we bring more wood with us. If we stay here unexpectedly, I send someone out with a load of wood to replenish it. We keep a plastic bin in the other part of the cave with blankets and canned food. I'll have to check it."

"So, who could be staying here without permission?" A

cold chill raced up her back.

"Hikers. Cattle rustlers. Some other criminal in need of a hideout."

Sam ran her light around the cave again. "Are we safe in here?" She stepped closer to Jake.

"I've got this with me." He patted his gun.

"Oh, yeah. I guess we are." She blew out a breath. "Okay, then. Show me around."

He took her hand as he walked toward the back. "There's a narrow passage back here."

They shuffled about forty feet down a twisting, turning tunnel then stepped into a larger cavern than the one at the cave entrance.

Jake's light made a quick sweep of the room and landed on the plastic bin.

Sam stepped beside him, moved her light around the walls. "Is this the end or is there another tunnel?"

"This is it. It's not that impressive, but I like it."

"I like it, too." She played her flashlight across the ceiling, made up of large slabs of rock. Her flashlight lit her path over mostly smooth rock to the center of the cavern.

Where the floor met the wall, the light caught something red. She focused her beam on it and approached it. Two backpacks. Her stomach clenched and she had to swallow a few times to prevent the bile from rising in her throat.

"Jake? Jake!"

He was beside her in an instant and stood between her and the opening to the tunnel. He must have thought she'd seen someone. He wrapped his arms around her. The chilled air of the cave wasn't what caused her shivers. It seemed unreasonable to react this way.

"Sammie, what's wrong?"

She pointed. "Jake, the backpacks. Th-the red one. It scares me."

One red and one kaki backpack leaned against the wall. Jake squatted in front of the packs. She stepped closer. Stuck on the flap of the red pack were hiking patches and a pin that read *Kiss Me I'm Irish*. Jake glanced up at her and his eyes narrowed.

He turned back to the bags, and unzipped the red one. He pulled clothes from the large compartment and stuffed them back in. He unzipped a pocket and pulled out handcuffs.

Sam gasped and he turned to her. She wrapped her arms around herself to stop the shivering. It didn't work. Her flashlight, now pointed at the ceiling, wavered. Tears filled her eyes and streaked down her cheeks. She didn't know why this intense fear had gripped her. She just knew she had to get away from this place.

"I'm sorry. I have to finish going through these packs." His arm dove into the tan bag, and something metallic rattled, but he didn't pull it out. He frowned when he reached into a small pocket, but didn't tell her what he'd found.

He stood, leaving the packs on the floor. "Sammie, we're getting out of here."

She nodded as Jake gave her a hug. His warmth invaded her but didn't replace the cold, then he led her back the way they'd come.

They mounted their horses. "All right, Sammie, go as fast as you can. I'll pace you."

Sam leaned close to Saffron's neck. "Let's go, girl." She gave a kick.

They raced across the field, Jake a bit behind her. Her breath came in short bursts and the poor horse was lathered, but she was too afraid to slow down. Jake edged ahead of her and signaled for her to slow down.

Sam caught her breath, and patted her horse. "You did good, girl."

She stared at Jake. "I don't understand what happened back there. Why was I so afraid of a backpack?"

Jake glanced at her and forward again. He didn't answer.

This felt like a tipping point. Something was on the edge of her memory and wanted out. She wanted it to stay in the dark. "There was more than just that accident and my father that caused my amnesia wasn't there?"

He sighed. "Yes, there was."

"Those backpacks belong to someone wh-who hurt me?" Her voice shook. If it was even her voice.

His lips pinched together, then he sighed. "It looks that way."

"Was I held captive?" She stared at Saffron's mane, waiting for him. "Jake?"

"Sammie, I think we should wait until we get back to the house before talking about this. Maybe we should have Dr. Reynolds come."

She stopped her horse.

He scanned the fields and settled his gaze on her.

"Jake. How long?"

He closed his eyes for a second then stared at her. "Three months. Now let's get moving again." He slapped Saffron's hip to get her in motion.

"I was a captive for three months? Why?"

"Sammie, when we get back."

She didn't really want to know. Why did she push it? The fear bubbling inside told her to back off. It would do her more harm than good to know anything about her missing past.

Chapter 16

At the door to the house, Jake stopped. "Sammie, please go into my office. I need to make a call and I'd really rather that you not hear about it yet, so I'm going to stay outside."

She stared into his eyes for several seconds then nodded and went inside.

Jake paced in the front yard. When he hadn't reached Alex on his office phone, he called his cell.

"Hey, Jake. What's up?"

"Sam and I ran into a situation on the ranch."

"What kind of situation?"

"We went for a ride to the cave. You remember it, don't you?"

"Oh, yeah. I prefer the hike in to the ride in. Three hours one way in a saddle was way too long. It's about a half-hour hike from the access road, right? What about it?"

"I took Sammie there this morning. It turns out someone's been using it. There were two backpacks there and the red one scared Sammie half to death. Both of them had handcuffs in them. I think they must belong to her kidnappers."

"That's awfully close to home. I'll go check on it right now. I can swab the cuffs; see if I can find hair. I think we should leave the bags there so they won't know we're onto them."

"I agree. Be careful. These guys are dangerous. They probably don't know that Sammie can't identify them. And if you come across them, I wouldn't blame you if you shot them. Just don't tell anyone I said that."

"I know what you mean, Jake. Those guys are the lowest of lowlifes. I'll let you know when I have info."

"And stake out the cave. One man, out of sight."

"Will do."

"Thanks, Alex."

He couldn't stay away from Sammie any longer. He joined her in his office, sat beside her on the couch and took her hand as he talked on the phone. "All right, Dr. Reynolds. Thanks for canceling your appointments. We'll see you in about an hour." He hung up the phone and pointed to Sam. "We will not discuss this until she gets here. I don't want to screw it up any more than I have already."

Jake couldn't take it anymore. Sammie's eyes were huge; she shivered. He pulled her onto his lap and hugged her. She wrapped her arms around him and snuggled her head under his chin. "Jake, I'm scared."

"I know you are, sunshine. I wish I could make this easier for you."

"You have. I can't imagine going through any of this without you."

He tipped her head up and kissed her. He wished there was more he could do. After many minutes her shivering subsided and she took a deep breath and relaxed. He almost thought she'd gone to sleep when the doorbell rang and she lifted her head.

He shifted her off his lap. "Be back in a minute."

He headed to the door, and pull it open. "Dr. Reynolds, thanks for coming so quickly. Sammie's really a mess after we found a backpack that she recognized."

Sam stood in the middle of the office, looking like a small, lost child. She held out her hand and Dr. Reynolds walked up to her and took it. "I'm glad you could come."

"I only had two appointments to reschedule and they

weren't emergencies. Where do you want to do this?" She scanned the office.

Sam said, "Should we pull another chair up to the table? Or should we go into the living room?"

"Where are you most comfortable, Sam?" asked Dr. Reynolds.

"Right here."

"Okay. Do you want Jake to stay?"

Sam looked up at him. "I need you here."

"Okay, then let's get started." They sat, the women facing each other and Jake on the end. "Ok, Sam. Let's start with when you first spotted the backpack."

"I was shining my light all around the cave. It was fun, interesting. Then I caught something red in the light and went back to it. I saw the backpacks. I was curious and started to walk toward them. When I got close enough I recognized the red one. It scared me. I didn't know where I'd seen it before, but I knew it was a bad place." Sam was kneading and squeezing her hands. Jake put a hand over hers and they stilled. She turned one hand up and took his. Moments later her hands relaxed.

Dr. Reynolds studied their hands and then Sam's face. "Okay, Sam, I want you to picture that backpack in a different setting. See the backpack and try to put it somewhere else you've seen it."

Jake gave Dr. Reynolds a startled look. This was such a bad idea. He didn't want her to remember the horrible things that had happened to her.

Sam's hands trembled in his, but she closed her eyes. Jake didn't think she was going to say anything, but finally she spoke.

"I can see it on a dirty, scarred hardwood floor, sitting beside a closed door. I see a rail type footboard and I'm sitting on a bed."

Her hands trembled again, but her eyes remained closed. "I don't think I can do this."

Dr. Reynolds spoke in a low, steady voice. "Sam, you're doing great. Can you look around the room? What else do you see?"

Her hands twitched. "I'm handcuffed to the bed. The only things in the room are the bed and the red backpack. I've stared at it for hours and I finally closed my eyes. The door slammed open and I jumped and open my eyes. By the time I see him his back is to me and he's squatted in front of the backpack. It looks like he stuffed something into it. He stands up and turns to me. He said, 'That idiot father of yours doesn't want to play with us. So, I guess we'll have to play with *you* for a while.' I-I made a noise and he-he swung his arm and back handed me."

Sam's hand flew to her cheek and she opened her eyes. "I can't, I don't want to remember any more of that." Tears were flowing down her cheeks. Jake squeezed her hand and when her eyes met his her hand stopped trembling. He hurt for her. He didn't want her to remember. What she'd remembered already was causing her too much pain. What would happen if she remembered the rest?

"Jake." When he turned to Dr. Reynolds, she asked, "What have you told Sam?"

"We were racing back here." Jake stared at their joined hands. "I wanted to get Sammie far away from that cave as quickly as possible. Then she stopped. She had figured out that she'd been kidnapped and wanted to know how long they held her captive. I didn't want to tell her, but she wouldn't move until I'd told her."

"And how long was it?" asked Dr. Reynolds quietly.

"We've estimated three months." His eyes turned back to Sammie. Tears ran down her cheeks.

"Jake, my father wouldn't pay my ransom. My own

father, who could have saved me, was responsible for whatever happened after that."

"I'm so sorry, sunshine. You didn't deserve what happened to you." Jake grabbed a box of tissues from his desk, and dropped it in front of Sam. She took one and wiped her face. Jake wished he was holding her right now.

"What now, Doctor?" Jake asked.

"I'd like to talk to Sam alone for a bit," Stacey said.

He looked into Sam's watery eyes. "Is that all right with you, Sammie?"

She bit her lip, but nodded.

"I'll be outside." Pacing.

After twenty minutes, the front door opened and he turned as Sammie and Dr. Reynolds walked across the porch and down the steps. He met them halfway to Dr. Reynolds' car.

She turned to Sam and said, "I'll be back in two days for your regularly scheduled visit, Sam. But call me if you can't wait that long. Now I want to talk to Jake alone."

"All right. I'll just go sit on the porch swing." She turned away.

Jake and Dr. Reynolds continued walking to her car. When they reached it, she turned to Jake and said in a loud accusing whisper, "You had sex with Sam."

Jake took a deep breath. He knew that's how she would see it. He'd considered calling Dr. Reynolds afterward but knew she'd misunderstand. "No, we made love. She asked me to and I couldn't refuse."

She frowned at him and started to speak.

Jake put up his hand and continued. "Sammie asked me to make love to her. I told her she wasn't ready for that. She got teary and said I wouldn't because her back was scarred. I felt at that point it would do her more harm to think that than it would to make love to her."

Stacey nodded. "I see your point, but I'm not happy about this."

Jake shrugged. "I know it might complicate things, but I *do* love her."

Stacey nodded again. "She hasn't had much love in her life. It's probably helped her more than anything that you were the one to find her, to be there for her. She considers you her savior and protector. I have to warn you that she may be responding to you as her protector. When she gets stronger, she might be ready to move on."

Dr. Reynolds drove away. He hoped that Sammie didn't consider him only her savior and protector. That's not how *he* felt. But if she decided it was time to leave, he'd find a way to accept it and let her move on. He ran a hand through his hair, turned and walked back to the porch.

Sam called out, "Jake, will you sit on the swing with me?"

"Whatever you want, Sammie." Jake sat and she curled up in his lap and tucked her head under his chin.

In a quiet voice, Sammie said, "I don't want to remember anything else, Jake. Except for Ben, anything I've remembered or been told has been a nightmare." She touched his cheek. "My life started when I woke to you holding my hand, heard you call me sunshine and when I opened my eyes and looked into your concerned face for the first time." Sam brought her face close to his and gave him a soft kiss. Before he could respond, she pulled back again and looked into his eyes. "I love you, Jake Hamilton."

She leaned forward to kiss him, and he cupped the back of her head. He wasn't ready for her to pull back again. This was going to be a long kiss. He let her give him another light kiss and then teased her lips with his tongue. She opened to him and he pulled her closer as he deepened the kiss. He'd only just recently realized how much she'd come to mean to him. At the office or on the road, his thoughts always turned to her. At the end of the day, his heart swelled with thoughts of Sammie. Some mornings it was hard to leave. He shared it all in his kisses.

Finally, he pulled back and touched his forehead to hers as their breathing slowly returned to normal. He tipped his head back so he could see her face. "I can't imagine a life here without you now. I'm always surrounded by people, so I didn't realize how lonely I'd been until you came here. You've become so important to me, sunshine."

Her stomach growled.

He chuckled. "I can see how much that meant to you."

She gave him a quick kiss. "It means everything to me, but we didn't get lunch. Let's go find food." She dipped her head and said in a quieter voice, "And then maybe you can help satisfy another hunger?"

Jake paused in helping Sam off his lap. First surprise registered and then a slow grin spread across his face. "Oh, I'm sure I can handle that."

Chapter 17

As Jake reached his office desk, the phone rang. "Sheriff Hamilton."

"Hi, Jake. It's Alex."

"Oh, Alex, do you have anything for me?" Jake dropped down in his chair.

"I searched both bags yesterday. Hair samples match one of the previous samples. I found partial prints on the handcuffs and took some blood samples from them. Sam definitely wore both pairs of cuffs."

Jake swore.

"I have a possible match on the prints. Thug by the name of Chuck Garr. Arrested for extortion, but got off. A few other petty things like bar fights."

"So why are they in a cave on *my* land?" asked Jake.

"Let's hope they don't know they're so close to Sam," Alex said. "They've probably figured that Sam could lead us back to the house where they were holding her and had to get out of there. Maybe they've hiked in the area and already knew about your cave."

"All right. Can you do a search to see if Chuck Garr owns property in the area? And if that doesn't pan out, check out abandoned houses within thirty miles of where Sammie crashed. I never considered that she might not have come far before she crashed."

"Okay. I'll get a team on it."

Jake leaned back in his chair. "I don't think we want an APB on Garr yet, but distribute his picture within the station.

Let them think we don't know about him yet. Maybe you can find out some more about him. Call me right away if anything comes up."

~~~

It was late afternoon when Alex called back. "Jake, one of the guys found a possible house. It's at least had squatters in it. I'm on my way out there now. Do you want to come?"

"Yeah. Give me the address; I'll drive separately."

A half-hour later, Jake pulled into the driveway behind Alex. The first cruiser was parked only about halfway up the drive. Alex waited for Jake to step up beside him. As they walked, they inspected the ground. "Looks like two different tire treads," said Alex.

"Can you get casts from these? One of them may be from the van Sammie used."

"That was my thought, too," Alex said.

They climbed the steps and talked to the officer standing at the door. "Good job finding this, John. I didn't see it from the road."

"Thank you, sir." The officer barely smiled.

Jake and Alex entered the house and both pulled on gloves and turned on flashlights. The living room was empty of everything except dirt. In the kitchen, putrefied garbage filled the trash can. Dirty pans overflowed the sink. The gas stove was covered with spilled food. A stack of paper plates sat on the counter. A cooler sat in front of a refrigerator. Jake opened it and dropped the lid back quickly. It was full of water and rotten food. "Woo. We're done in the kitchen."

They checked the rest of the first floor and didn't find anything useful. Jake turned to Alex. "Upstairs or down, Alex?"

"Most likely they held her in the basement; so let's look

there first. Alex led the way. They played their flashlights over everything.

Jake shook his head. "I don't think they've been down here."

"No, so let's try the second floor." Alex again led the way. They stepped into the first bedroom. A mattress was on the floor with sheets on it. Discarded pieces of clothing and paper plates with remnants of a meal lay beside it.

In the next room, a mattress rested on a bed frame. Jake examined the white painted metal headboard with its chipped paint. The floor behind the bed was covered with flecks of paint. "I think this is where Sammie was cuffed. Paint is chipped on a couple of the bars." Jake tried to ignore the dirty, stained sheets and the plastic bucket beside the bed with the stench of urine. He fisted his hand. If Alex wasn't there, he would have punched the wall. These animals needed to pay for what they'd done to her. He stepped back to the doorway, closed his eyes, and took deep breaths until his emotions were under control. He opened his eyes and found Alex watching him.

"You've gotten close to her, haven't you?" Alex asked.

"Yeah. I hate what happened to her." Jake dragged in another breath. "Have these sheets analyzed, Alex."

Jake surveyed the room again, and spotted a black handle sticking out from behind the door. He moved the door with his foot. It was a hammer. The head was covered in blood and hair. "Well, look what we have here. Maybe the guys had a falling out." Jake turned to Alex. "Check this for blood and prints."

They found nothing in the bathroom. The third bedroom was very much like the first.

This time Jake led the way. "I want to have a look out back. I assume they parked behind the house to hide their vehicles. Maybe they dropped something." Jake and Alex combed the ground around the places where the tire tracks ended. Other than trash, they didn't find anything useful.

"Hey, Alex. Does it look like the ground has been disturbed over there?"

Alex headed toward it. "Yeah, I think you're right." New, but sparse weeds had started to grow over the two by four foot area.

Jake tipped his head. "Do you have a couple of shovels?"

"I've got one. I'll see if John has one."

Alex returned within a few minutes with two shovels. He handed one to Jake. "Let's do this carefully. We don't want to damage any evidence." Instead of digging deep in one spot, they kept the depth of the hole level.

After the hole was a little over a foot deep, Alex said, "I hit something." They stuck their shovels into the pile of dirt they'd made, and knelt beside the hole, carefully scooping dirt with their hands.

Jake paused. "I've got a head here." They worked to clear dirt from around it. When they'd uncovered enough, Jake sat back, taking shallow breaths. Between the smell and the misshapen head, he feared he'd lose his last meal. A patch of scruffy hair on the face suggested it was male. "My guess is the hammer we found upstairs is what killed him."

Jake checked his watch. It was approaching six-thirty. He should have been on his way home by now. "I'll call the M.E. While you're waiting for him, can you get casts of the tires and prints throughout the house?"

Alex nodded.

"And don't forget to bag the hammer."

Alex gave him a surprised look.

"Sorry. I know you would have anyway. If you don't mind, I'm going home. I'll tell John he can leave when the M.E. gets here."

"All right. See you tomorrow, Jake."

Jake drove home, anxious for the scene to be processed, so he could get the information from it and the M.E.'s report before talking to Sam about it. *If* he talked to her about it. It upset her too much seeing a backpack. He'd get Alex's opinion about it when he called with his report.

Chapter 18

Jake set lunch and a cup of coffee on his desk and dropped into the chair. He wondered how Sammie was doing. He'd told Paul about the possible criminal hiding out in the cave and that if Sam went riding, she was to go no more than an hour out in any other direction. He should have told her she couldn't go out at all.

He opened the bag when Alex stuck his head around the door. "You have time to talk?"

"This isn't going to spoil my lunch, is it?"

"It might. Do you want me to come back?"

"No, come on in," Jake said with resignation. "Do you want half a sandwich? I have a feeling I won't be able to eat it all. But you can't have my pickle."

Alex sat. "Thanks." He picked up half a sub after Jake tore the paper it sat on and slid it closer to Alex.

"First off—"

Jake raised a hand and cut him off.

"We're eating before I hear this. So, tell me how little Alexis is doing?"

Alex smiled. "She's great! She took her first steps this past weekend. I missed the first time she got on her hands and knees and stood on her own. So, it was fun to watch her working on those steps and see her excitement when she did it."

Jake smiled. An image of a toddler with Sammie's eyes doing the same thing popped into his head. He needed to keep her safe so they could have that life.

Jake packed away the remnants of lunch and dropped it in the trash. "All right, what do you have?"

"One set of tire tracks match the van Sam drove."

"That wasn't a surprise."

"Doors, doorknobs, banister, bed rails, kitchen counters were all wiped."

"Damn!" Jake had hoped they'd slipped up, but there was still the body with its prints.

"I did find one good hand print on a wall. It wasn't helpful. It belonged to the dead guy, who also matches the partial print on the cuffs. So we still don't know who the other man is."

Jake frowned. They needed another break.

"The DNA suggests the two are related. Can you find out if Garr has a brother, half-brother, uncle or cousin he worked with?"

"I'll see what I can find out when we notify next of kin." Alex wrote down some notes. "Now the hammer." He paused.

"Go on. What about it? Was it the murder weapon?"

"The M.E. confirmed that the hammer was used to kill Garr. I wouldn't call it murder." He stopped speaking.

Jake stared at him. What did he mean by that? If it wasn't murder—it hit him. Self defense. "Sammie did it?"

Alex nodded. "There are smudged prints on the hammer. Presumably one or both of the men. But the ones on top are very clear and they're Sam's." In a quieter voice, Alex said, "The M.E. said that he was hit as least six times."

Jake closed his eyes and ran a hand through his hair. Sammie had another reason for not wanting to remember. He could imagine the kind of nightmares she would have if she remembered hitting Garr over and over with a hammer. And if she remembered that, she would surely remember what they'd done to her. Jake opened his eyes. "And if these two men are related, he not only wants to eliminate Sammie because he thinks she can identify him, he wants revenge."

"If he's on your property he may have seen her already. I think we should put a team of two on the cave."

"Can you set it up?"

Alex stood. "I'll work out the details and let you know."

"Thanks."

An hour later, Alex called. "Jake, the first team of two will arrive in about an hour. One will stay in the cave and the other outside. The first officers were dropped so, they'll leave in the car the next two come in. In six hours, two more will replace them. I think we should only do this for three days tops. If the guy doesn't show up by then, he's found a new place to hide."

As Jake was leaving for the day, his cell phone rang. It was Paul. His foreman knew how to handle almost anything, so rarely called him at the office. He was afraid to receive the call, but had to. "Hey, Paul. What's up?"

"Jake." His voice was near panic.

It was bad.

"Sam and Adam went for a ride this afternoon. Adam's horse just came back."

"What?" Stay calm. He needed to think. "Call everybody who's out and have them start looking for them. Remember, there's a dangerous guy out there. If anybody's still at the barn, have them take the pick-ups. I'm on my way."

As he left, he called Alex from his cell. "Alex, Sammie and Adam went out for a ride and Adam's horse just came in. Can you let the men know? I'm headed out to the cave."

"I'll join you out there."

Chapter 19

They were almost to the river when chills ran up Sam's spine. Something wasn't right. It felt like someone was watching them. She checked in all directions, but didn't see anything suspicious. "Adam?"

He glanced her way.

"I think we should head back. Something's—"

A shot rang out and Adam fell to the ground. Sam screamed and edged her horse over to Adam's and gave it a slap. It took off. She hoped it would go back to the barn.

A hand snaked out and snatched the horse's reins from her. Something hard pressed into her ribs.

"Damn."

A voice from her nightmares made her tremble. She closed her eyes. It couldn't be real.

"I was going to use that horse. I guess we'll have to snuggle up on yours. Get your foot out of the stirrup."

Sam froze. What was he going to do? She thought she should know, but she didn't want to. He seemed familiar, but she blocked all thoughts that would let her remember.

"Now!" he yelled. She moved her foot and he mounted behind her. "Now isn't this cozy? I didn't expect you to be so close by."

"Please don't hurt me. I don't remember what happened. I haven't seen you now. You could just leave me here and get away."

"Oh, no. I have plans for you," he said in a soothing voice. Then it turned hard. "You're going to pay for killing my brother."

"No! I didn't kill anyone. I couldn't." She covered her ears. She didn't want to hear his lies.

The man grabbed her hair and yanked her head back. Her hands slipped from her head. The horse danced and nickered. "Conveniently forgotten, huh? Well, let me refresh your memory. Somehow you got loose and found a hammer."

Sam trembled. Tears filled her eyes and spilled over. No. All this should stay buried.

"You must have hid behind the door and when Chucky walked in, you hit him on the head."

"No!" Sam screamed and struggled.

He slammed the gun into her ribs. "You hit him over and over until he was dead." He yelled and she wished it was loud enough someone would hear.

Then he spoke in a quieter voice, an almost reasonable sounding voice, except for the words he used. "So now I'm going to make you hurt so bad you'll wish you were dead. Then I'm going to give you your wish." He laughed.

Sam didn't remember. She didn't want to. But she wondered what horrible things happened that she would be able to kill. It was better to think that somebody else had done it. She trembled and he laughed again.

~~~

Jake pulled into the access road right behind Alex. He got out of the car and his phone rang. It was Paul. He hoped Sammie and Alex were both found unharmed. "Find anything, Paul?"

"Yeah. Steve just found Adam. He was almost to the river. He was shot through the arm. Nothing vital hit. Steve's bringing him to the house and Abby will run him to the hospital while Steve goes back out again."

Jake ran his free hand through his hair. "So, it's really him. What did Adam have to say?"

"They were taken by surprise. He didn't see anyone before he passed out."

"Does he know what time he got shot?" Jake asked.

"I didn't think to ask," Paul said. "But Sam and Adam left the barn about one. They would have got to where Adam was found about two. So I'd guess she's been with that guy for a couple of hours."

"Thanks, Paul. That helps." Jake set his phone to vibrate and dropped it back into his pocket as he told Alex about Adam.

He had to maintain control. He was the sheriff, and protected people every day. He had to think straight in order to save the woman he loved. "If he's bringing her to the cave, then they should be there in about an hour."

"Hopefully he doesn't realize the cave is under surveillance," Alex said. "Let's go. If they don't show as expected, we'll start a new search from there." He placed calls to the men monitoring the cave to let them know that the guy could be there soon with Sam.

Jake and Alex worked their way up the path that led to the cave. They found a place to hide with a view of the approach to the cave.

Twenty minutes later, a horse appeared in the distance. As it got closer, Jake recognized Sam. Closer still, Jake could see that the man held a gun in one hand. He slowed the horse to a walk and rounded the tree in front of the cave entrance. The man dismounted and held the reins, pointing the gun at Sam. It was Gerald Wilder, Chuck Garr's half brother.

"Get off and don't try anything."

She slid down and stood facing the horse with her head bowed while the man tied the reins to a tree branch.

He pushed the gun into her back and she gasped. His other hand dug into her forearm. "Now march into the cave."

Jake was torn up inside. The woman he loved might be dead in the next few minutes. His heart pounded. They couldn't rush the guy because he'd pull the trigger. His only hope was Jim would be able to take the man by surprise.

Jake waited until they entered the cave, and was sure they'd had started down the tunnel, then he stood. Alex looked up at him, eyes wide.

Jake mouthed, "I'm going in."

Alex shook his head, but Jake started walking. He placed each foot with care. He didn't want to snap a twig or rustle leaves. When he stood beside the cave, he stopped and peeked around the edge of the opening.

The first room was empty. Most of the floor was dirt, so it would be easier to be quiet. He crept toward the tunnel and paused at the entrance to listen. Sammie's rapid breathing told him how scared she was. He wished she didn't have to go through this again. Be a captive again. Did it bring back those horrible memories?

Jake started down the tunnel. Most of the floor was rock, so he put his foot down slowly. Sound traveled well through the passage, and he didn't want to alert the man. He was about a third of the way through when Sammie screamed and men yelled.

Then a gun went off. Pulling his flashlight out, he ran.

He stopped at the entrance to the second room and surveyed the scene. The light from a flashlight on the floor shone on the far wall. There was a scuffle to the right and he turned his light there. Jim and the man were struggling on the floor. Where was Sam? He shone his light around and found her to his left, with her back pressed to the wall.

She was standing. Alive. A cool balm bathed him.

Jake turned his light back to the men and hurried toward

them. Halfway there, another gunshot echoed. He ran and pulled the men apart. Jim sucked in gulps of air. The other man didn't move. Jake kicked away the gun on the floor. He knelt and felt for a pulse. He didn't find one and the air whooshed out of his lungs. Maybe this was over.

He glanced at Sammie. She needed him. Even though the danger was past, her eyes were still huge with fear.

He turned to the man beside him, "You okay, Jim?"

"Yeah, Sheriff, but it was close."

Jake squeezed Jim's shoulder. "You did good." A noise behind him made him stand and spin around, his gun in front of him.

Alex raised his hands. "We all good in here?"

Jake let his breath out and holstered his gun. "The good guys are good." He rushed to Sammie, pulled her into a hug, and she wrapped her arms around his waist like she would never let go. He held his life in his arms. He couldn't imagine living without her. He'd come too close to losing her. He held her closer.

"Jake, you found me. I thought I was going to die." She shivered.

"Let's get you out of here and into the sunshine, sunshine." Jake tried to pull away from her but she held tighter. "Sammie, you have to let go. We won't both fit through the tunnel. Give me your hand. I won't let go."

She held tight for a few more seconds then slid one hand from behind Jake and he caught it with his. Then she removed her other arm from around him. He kissed her forehead. "Okay, let's go."

Back in the sunshine, Jake wrapped her back in his arms, and she clung to him. She pressed her cheek to his chest and the words rushed out through her tears. "Jake, he said I killed his brother. He said that he was going to hurt me so bad that I'd wish I was dead and then he'd grant my wish. Jake—"

He lifted her chin, then put a finger on her lips. "Shh. Let's talk about this later." He tightened his arms around her and tucked her head under his chin. He didn't want to ever let her go. "You're safe now. Let's get you back to the house."

Sirens blared in the distance. His head snapped around when there was movement beside him. "Ah, Alex."

"Didn't mean to startle you. I'll take care of the team. Why don't you get out of here?"

"Thanks. Come by when this is taken care of."

Alex walked down the path.

Jake untied the horse, and slapped its hip. "Go on home, Saffron."

"Will she be okay?" Sam watched the horse gallop away.

"She knows her way home. Jax got home fine and that alerted Paul that something was wrong. It's a good thing he got away."

"I-I did that. I thought it might slow us down if we had only one horse."

Jake pulled her toward him until their bodies touched. He kissed her forehead. "You did good." He blinked back the tears in his eyes. He dragged in a shaky breath. "I hope you can do a half hour walk to the car."

"I can." Her voice was stronger. "Just don't let go of me."

They met the team half-way down the path and stepped to the side to let several men and a stretcher pass. They finished the trek and Jake helped her into the car. Fortunately, it wasn't blocked in by the emergency vehicles. He had them on the road in just a few minutes with the heat blasting, to warm her.

Jake swore and Sam raised her eyebrows. He smiled. "It's okay. I just forgot something." He pulled out his cell phone and dialed. "Paul, call in the hands. Sam is safe. Saffron is on her way back on her own, so keep an eye out for her. And thank them all for me."

"She's okay? That's great."

"Yeah, it is."

Sam put her hand on his thigh. "You had everybody out looking for me? Thank you."

He raised his eyebrows. "Of course I did." He lifted her hand and kissed it. "You're everything to me. I couldn't lose you."

They strode through the front door of the house, and Abby stepped into the hall from the kitchen.

Jake grinned at her. "Sammie's fine. Everybody's coming in."

"Good," She rushed up to Sam and threw her arms around her. "I'm glad you're safe. I've got stew, when you're ready." Then she returned to the kitchen.

Chapter 20

Sammie let Jake pull her up the stairs, and into his bedroom. He closed the door, and led her to the bathroom. She was all for it. She was still chilled and shivering. He turned on the water then fumbled with the buttons on Sammie's shirt, and must have given up. He pulled her shirt open and buttons bounced across the floor. He dropped it in the trash. Then he helped her step out of her pants and dropped them in the trash.

Sam clasped his hands. She knew what he was doing. "Jake my underwear doesn't have to go in the trash. My pants don't have to go in the trash."

He leaned his forehead against hers and took a deep breath. "Okay." He helped her remove the rest of her clothes and dropped them on the floor. He adjusted the water and Sam stepped under the flow. She closed her eyes and tipped her head back, allowing the water to flow through her hair and down her back. Warmth seeped into her and the water cleansed her. That man's hands on her had sent fear spiking through her. She'd known there would be pain.

She jumped when Jake's hand touched her arm. He stood naked in front of her. She smiled. This was what she needed. This man. He picked up the soap and they took turns cleaning the horror of the day from each other.

He turned off the water and grabbed fluffy, yellow towels from the towel bar. He wrapped one around her and dried himself.

She stepped out of the tub, rubbed the towel over

herself, and dropped it. She wrapped her arms around him. "Jake, I need you. Make love to me."

He picked her up, carried her to the bed, and set her on her feet beside the bed. "Are you sure? We can just snuggle."

After the day's trauma, that's what she should do, but she needed more. Jake would make her feel normal again. "I'm sure."

He pulled back the covers and helped her slide to the center of the bed. He retrieved a small packet from the nightstand, then slid into the bed beside her. His lips claimed hers as his hands gave her body new things to remember.

A long while later Sam relaxed in Jake's arms. Her life felt right again. He ran his hand up and down her arm. There was a lot that could be said for snuggling. She'd needed the lovemaking for so many reasons, but now, they fit together perfectly.

He sighed.

She frowned and ran a finger down his cheek. "What was that for?"

"Alex is coming, if he isn't here already. We should get dressed and meet him."

She scanned the room, "Except I don't have anything in here to put on."

He smiled. "For now you can wear my robe to get to your room. I think tomorrow we should move all your stuff into here."

She kissed him. "I'd like that." She scampered off the bed, claimed his robe then slipped out of the room. It took her a few minutes to dress and brush out her hair.

She found Jake talking to Abby in the kitchen.

Abby wrapped her in a hug. "Jake just told me what happened. I'm glad you're okay. I was so worried."

"Thank you." She got the feeling that she wasn't used to people caring about her.

"The men should be back any time now," Jake said.

Sam gasped. "I forgot about Adam!"

Jake squeezed her hand. "He's okay. When his horse came back, Paul sent everybody out and they found him pretty quickly. He hit his head on a rock when he fell and he was just coming around when they found him. They brought him back and Abby took him to the hospital. It was a clean shot through the arm. It didn't hit bone. They'll probably release him tomorrow."

"Oh, thank God. I can't believe that I was so wrapped up in myself that I didn't even think about him."

Jake kissed her cheek. "You can't call what happened to you today, being wrapped up in yourself. It's late. Are you ready to eat?" She nodded, and they went to the counter where the aroma from a pot of stew made her stomach rumble.

They were halfway through the meal when the doorbell rang. Abby rushed off to answer it and brought Alex back to the kitchen.

"Take some food and have a seat, Alex." Jake pointed to the counter.

"Thanks. It's been a long afternoon." Alex quickly filled his bowl and sat down across from them.

They ate as they talked. The first ranch hand straggled in and ladled some stew.

Alex said, "It turns out this guy was a half brother to Chuck Garr. His name was—"

"Jerry," Sam interrupted. Both men stared at her.

"Gerald Wilder. Four years older than Chuck. Do you remember him, Sam?" Alex asked.

She shook her head. "No, but when you said Chuck, it just popped into my head."

Jake's hand had been resting on her thigh and he squeezed it. She loved his silent support.

"Alex, Gerald said that I killed his brother. Did I?" She needed to know but she didn't want to if it meant that it was true.

His gaze strayed to Jake.

Jake clasped her hand. A very bad sign. "Sammie."

She turned to him, every muscle tense.

"You did what you had to do to survive. If you hadn't killed him and escaped, you would be—" He didn't finish. She knew he couldn't say it. He tucked her head under his chin, and kissed the top of her head.

Sam rested there for a few seconds, absorbing Jake's love, then pulled back. "Am I in trouble?"

Jake frowned.

Alex said, "I've already talked to the D.A. It was clearly self defense, so no charges will be filed against you."

"Thank you, Alex. Is this really over?"

"It's as over as you want it to be, Sam." He stood. "Now I have to get home."

~~~

"I'll walk you to the door." Jake rounded the table. They went outside and he closed the door. "Usually I don't want the perp to end up dead, but in this case, it saves Sammie from hearing in court everything that happened to her."

"She still doesn't remember much from before?"

"Almost nothing about the kidnapping. Bits and pieces about the rest of her life. Somewhat more about her brother. He was the only person in her life who really cared what happened to her."

Alex squeezed Jake's shoulder. "Well, she's got lots of people who care about her now. See you later, Jake."

"Bye, Alex. And thanks." Jake went back inside the house.

Sam came towards him. He took a few steps forward and waited. He loved watching her.

She stopped in front of him and took his hand. "I've been racking my brain, but I can't figure this out. What did Alex mean when he said it was as over as *I* want it to be?" She frowned at him and tipped her head.

Jake kissed her lips and studied her. "I think he meant that you can keep trying to remember what happened to you or you can go forward from here and live your new life."

She touched his cheek. Her eyes were bright with unshed tears. "I did remember something else. I rarely dated and I never let anyone get close. I was always afraid for anyone to see my back. And I was afraid that he would turn out to be like my father."

He kissed her palm.

"Without my memory, I didn't know at first that I had those scars. I started to fall for you. Then when we found them, it didn't matter to you."

"I wouldn't say it doesn't matter."

She frowned.

"I hate your father for doing that to you. I hate that it affected your life. But those scars do not define you any longer."

She smiled. Something wonderful had come out of the terrible events she'd gone through.

"I love who you are." He pulled her against him. "I love your body."

She kissed his chin.

He nibbled her earlobe. "Were you on your way upstairs?"

She nodded and surprised him when she pulled out of his arms, raced up the stairs and into his room. He chuckled and chased after her, closing his door and stared at the bathroom door. What was she doing in there? He kicked off his shoes and leaned against the hallway door, a smile curved his lips as he waited for Sam to appear.

After not much more than a minute, the bathroom door opened just a crack and Sam peeked around the edge of the door. She bit her lip and then slowly opened it the rest of the way. She stood framed in the doorway in a white teddy that left nothing to the imagination. He straightened up from the door, whistled then smiled. "Wow! When did you get that?"

"A couple of days ago I went into town with Abby. I-I had to borrow some of the grocery money to buy it. Do you mind?"

He glanced at his pants just below his belt. "You have to ask?"

She giggled nervously and sauntered toward him. She did an exaggerated hip swing that made his mouth dry. When she reached him, she started to unbutton his shirt, pulled it open and kissed his chest. He sucked in a breath. She pulled the shirt out of his pants and pushed it off his shoulders. He reached between them and unbuttoned the cuffs and let the shirt slide to the floor.

In a raspy voice, he said, "You do realize you aren't going to wear that very long, don't you?"

"Yeah, but I figured it would be long enough to get the effect I wanted." She tipped her head up and kissed the spot where his neck met his shoulder. Her tongue darted out and licked it.

His arms wrapped around her. "And what effect is that?" He barely got the words out.

She tipped her head up to his ear. "This is sort of a celebration. I'm free of my past and I want to make love with you because I *want* to make love with you."

He squinted down at her. "That doesn't make sense."

She stretched up and gave him a quick kiss on the lips. She closed her eyes for a couple of seconds then met his gaze. "Every time we've made love so far, I've needed it for something. I needed reassurance. I was scared. I was worried. I was sad." She frowned and rushed on. "Don't misunderstand me. You're the only one I needed, the only one who could do this for me." She kissed him again. "But this time, the *only* reason I want to make love with you is that I love you. Now I think you should take me over to that bed." Her eyes flicked to the bed and back to him.

He took her lips in a searing kiss and lifted her off the floor. He laid her on the bed and gave her another kiss. "I love you more than you know. I'm so glad I found you, today *and* months ago."

He stood and stripped off the rest of his clothes and she pulled him down next to her.

Chapter 21

Jake watched Sammie sleep. The morning light made a halo in her hair. The dark circles under her eyes were gone. She was beautiful. His life had changed so much when she entered it. He kept so busy he hadn't realized how lonely he'd been. Coming home to Sammie each work day was a joy. The excitement he felt as he got closer to the ranch, made him realize how empty his life had been, doing what needed to be done.

Her eyes opened and he smiled. "Good morning, sunshine."

She kissed her fingertips, touched his lips with them. "Good morning."

He kissed her fingers, then clasped her hand. "I was thinking." He paused.

"That's a good thing to do."

When he still didn't continue, she raised her eyebrows and he smiled. "I think we should invite Ben to visit again in about a month."

"I'd like that."

"Yeah, I'm sure you would want your brother at your wedding." Jake watched her.

It took a full two seconds before her eyes widened in surprise. Her upper body flew toward him and she wrapped her arms around his neck and kissed him. She leaned back, dragging him with her.

Jake pulled away far enough to see her face. "I'm so crazy in love with you that I can't imagine my life without you."

Sam smiled and lifted her head to kiss him then dropped it back down on the pillow. "I can't imagine my life without you either. Of course, the only part of my life I remember are the ones that include you." She gave him a smile that made his stomach flip. "Now show me."

THE END

Books by Deborah Wallace

Wounded Warrior Hearts Series
Wounded Warrior Hearts: Steven
Wounded Warrior Hearts: Amy
Wounded Warrior Hearts: Russ

Rawlins Series
Kathleen's Legacy
Jason's Forbidden Woman
Jamie's Trials
Adam's Redemption
Kristy's Puzzle

Choice Series
Second Choice
Third Choice – *Fall 2020*
No Choice – *Winter 2020*

Other Books
I Shot the Sheriff
New Memories
Father Unknown
Only My Love

Check out my website for details on these books and where
to find them. You can also sign up to receive emails when I
have a new book. www.DeborahWallaceBooks.com.

You can also find them on Amazon.
amazon.com/author/deborahwallacebooks

If you can take the time, I'd love if you left a review of my book on your favorite Book sites. Thank you.

About Deborah Wallace

Someone suggested I try writing, and stories started populating my brain, begging to be put on paper (or my computer screen).

I've got quite a number of books under my belt, but the ones I keep coming back to are the romantic suspense. When I wrote the first *Rawlins* book, I thought it would be the only paranormal. Then I said 'what if...' and now children of the first characters and a couple of friends have books.

I have been called a Jane-of-all-trades, from seamstress to house and furniture designer/builder to computer programmer to technical writer and bookkeeper. I even do car maintenance. I've also guided a team of 'Future Problem Solvers'.

I grew up in Michigan, but Massachusetts has been my home for more years than I care to think about. I love the history here, the museums and antique houses, the seacoast and hiking trails.

My three children have grown and scattered, but my husband is by my side, encouraging my writing.